"My child will not be born a bastard."

The blood drained from Mia's face, leaving the honey gold of her skin washed out. "What?"

"That is not acceptable. This child will be born in wedlock and inherit everything that is rightfully his or hers."

"You've lost your mind."

The more her panic rose, as she stood straight and stiff like a glass pane about to break, the more Nikandros's own resolve solidified. The restlessness that had clawed at him all these months... Was this the answer?

He'd realized the daredevil lifestyle had begun to lose its glitter.

Was it time for a new direction in his life?

An attraction that defied all the usual conventions and a child on the way—was it enough to make a marriage?

It had to be. For he could never walk away from his own child. And this was not an impulse. Or a challenge. This was the only rational way forward. For both of them.

"No, I've never actually been this lucid before. We will marry as soon as possible."

The Drakon Royals

Royalty never looked this scandalous!

To the outside world, the Drakon Royals have the world at their feet. Yet beneath the surface, black-hearted Crown Prince Andreas, his daredevil younger brother Prince Nikandros and their illegitimate sister Princess Eleni hide the secrets of their family name...

Until one brush with desire, and each Drakon finds themselves at the heart of their very own scandal!

Find out what happens in:

Crowned for the Drakon Legacy
April 2017

The Drakon Baby Bargain
June 2017

Look out for Andreas and Ariana's story
August 2017

You won't want to miss this outrageously scandalous new trilogy from Tara Pammi!

Tara Pammi

CROWNED FOR THE DRAKON LEGACY

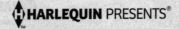

HARLEQUIN PRESENTS®

Recycling programs
for this product may
not exist in your area.

ISBN-13: 978-0-373-06059-7

Crowned for the Drakon Legacy

First North American Publication 2017

Copyright © 2017 by Tara Pammi

This edition published by arrangement with Harlequin Books S.A.

For questions and comments about the quality of this book,
please contact us at CustomerService@Harlequin.com.

® and TM are trademarks of Harlequin Enterprises Limited or its
corporate affiliates. Trademarks indicated with ® are registered in the
United States Patent and Trademark Office, the Canadian Intellectual
Property Office and in other countries.

Printed in U.S.A.

Tara Pammi can't remember a moment when she wasn't lost in a book—especially a romance, which was much more exciting than a mathematics textbook at school. Years later, Tara's wild imagination and love for the written word revealed what she really wanted to do. Now she pairs alpha males who think they know everything with strong women who knock that theory *and* them off their feet!

Books by Tara Pammi

Harlequin Presents

The Sheikh's Pregnant Prisoner
The Man to Be Reckoned With
A Deal with Demakis

Brides for Billionaires

Married for the Sheikh's Duty

The Legendary Conti Brothers

The Surprise Conti Child
The Unwanted Conti Bride

Greek Tycoons Tamed

Claimed for His Duty
Bought for Her Innocence

Society Weddings

The Sicilian's Surprise Wife

A Dynasty of Sand and Scandal

The Last Prince of Dahaar
The True King of Dahaar

Visit the Author Profile page at Harlequin.com for more titles.

For Pippa—Thank you for everything!

CHAPTER ONE

A BANKER NAMED Melissa from LA...

A concierge named Chloe in a swanky country club in Manhattan...

A cocktail waitress...

Mia Rodriguez scrolled down her cell phone screen, bile rising in her throat.

The list of her dead husband's affairs was endless.

The throaty purr of the fiery red exclusive sports car was like a faint echo as it put distance between her and the hungry horde of reporters.

In the blink of an eye, the press conference to announce her retirement from soccer had turned into a circus with Brian's infidelities taking center stage. A year since his death and he was still haunting her.

Fingers shaking, she pressed the little flickering triangle on a video.

Brian was voracious when it came to sex...

Every time we met, he wore me out...

His wife, Mia, probably only had time for soccer, and it's obvious Brian turned to me for what he didn't get from her...

"Turn it off."

She squeezed her eyes closed. Tears would have been a relief; tears would have meant that she could vent the tumult building up inside. Tears would mean that she felt something, anything for the man she'd married.

The anchor's voice etched into her mind as the clip played again and again.

Mia Rodriguez was not woman enough for her husband—

"Turn that blasted thing off."

The shuddering halt of the powerful engine pitched Mia toward the dashboard. She gasped at the tight pull of the seat belt against her chest. Her heart catapulted into her throat. Large, unfamiliar hands grabbed her cell phone and tossed it onto the backseat.

Mia followed the motion like a doll, the flickering screen sliding against the buttery leather.

"Mia…look at me."

She raised her confused gaze from the fingers on her chin at the commanding tone.

Intense blue eyes collided with hers, driving the breath out of her lungs. A strong, aquiline nose; a wide, languid, laughing mouth; a face that made women over the world swoon and sigh. Such a man and so close…

Not just any man. *A prince.* Lethal masculinity and pulse-pounding charm.

Nikandros Drakos.

Daredevil Prince of Drakon, second in line to the throne, extreme adventure sport enthusiast and sexy as sin…

Intending to push him away, she wrapped her fingers

around his wrist. Hair-roughened skin scraped the pads of her fingers, rough and tantalizing, so wholly alien to her own... A jolt of lightning jump-started every neuron, wakened every cell from a deep, slumbering haze.

Her gaze moved to the long fingers gripping the steering wheel. From there, she followed the veins on the back of his hands to his wrists.

A Patek Philippe watch sat on his right wrist, its big dial winking at her in the low light. A sportsman's watch. She'd been given one too, when their team had won the world championship four years ago. When Nikandros had still owned the team.

Her gaze crawled up until it reached the breadth of his shoulders, the angle of his jaw, the slightly long, dark hair curling at his collar...

"Stop listening to those horrid little interviews."

She blinked and looked away.

He seemed huge, overwhelmingly male and far too close in the dark confines of the car. He'd been Brian's close friend. A man she'd come to loathe, for her reckless husband had worshipped him as if he were truly his liege.

A man who had always made his opinion, that Mia wasn't good enough for Brian, crystal clear. A man who was addicted to the thrill that came from taunting death in the face. A man with no control over his thrill-seeking impulses.

Everything Mia abhorred in a man.

The fiery resentment spurred her out of her choking self-pity.

But nothing could dim her awareness of the man

waiting, far too close for comfort, and watching her from those intense blue eyes.

The silence took on a tangible quality, a jeering voice betraying her body's near-violent reaction to him. God, she'd die if he guessed it. Even this humiliation in front of the entire world, this mockery she was being made of by the media, would still be less painful than seeing the cool, contemptuous dismissal of those ice-blue eyes.

The thought snapped her spine into place.

This awareness was a reaction to shock, a basic human need for touch in the face of adversity.

It had been months, no, three years, since a man had even touched her.

Accepting that piece of truth pumped courage into her veins.

She stared through the windshield, only now taking in their surroundings.

They had left downtown Miami behind and had reached a swanky, luxury neighborhood. The high-rise apartment complex visible from the car made this whole situation even more surreal.

She barely met his gaze, and then turned, faking interest in the surroundings. "Sorry, I should've given you directions. It's going back for you but I'd appreciate it if you'd drop me at my apartment." Good, she sounded steady, polite.

"I believe your mother and sister live in Houston, yes?"

Startled that he knew that much, she nodded. It seemed a live current pulsed to life every time their eyes met. Mia had never thought antipathy could become so tangible between two people.

"I can have the pilot fuel the jet and drop you off."

If Brian and she had been minor celebrities with soccer fans, this man was royalty himself. He owned private jets, soccer teams and Extreme Adventure Clubs, and this was when the tabloids didn't count the wealth he'd inherited as the scion of the powerful royal house of Drakon.

The Prince who had thrown away his legacy...

"That's not necessary," she managed to say. Every time he spoke, that deep voice jolted places inside of her Mia had forgotten even existed. "You've done far too much already."

"You speak as if I were one of those jackals back at the press meet, as if I were the enemy too." A hint of impatience and something else peeked through in his voice. As if something more than years-old animosity existed between them.

He was a prince—privileged in every way possible, handsome, reckless, charming, without an ounce of substance.

She—everything she had in life she'd worked damned hard for. She didn't know when the last time she'd done anything that had amounted to fun had been. The career she'd worked toward for her whole life was over at twenty-six.

They had nothing in common.

This whole line of conversation was far too personal for her comfort. "I don't know you enough for you to engender such strong emotion."

"Mia Rodriguez Morgan does not show emotion, does she? I forget your reputation."

"You know nothing of me except for the persona created by the media, Your Highness. Your friendship with Brian tells you nothing about me."

"You're right. I do not know you." There was that note of annoyance in his tone again. "Tell me, should I call the pilot then?"

"Thanks for the offer. But I'll just call a cab." She reached between their seats and stretched her hand to grab her cell. "If you can wait till the cab gets here, I'd appreciate it. I don't want to wait on this stretch alone."

"I would appreciate if you would do me the courtesy of looking at me when I speak to you, Mia. We've known each other for a decade."

"And we've disliked each other for the whole damned decade, so please, let's not pretend otherwise."

A stillness filled the car at Mia's outburst.

He was right. She'd met him before she'd even met Brian. She'd been seventeen, playing for the junior team when she'd met the young European Prince of Drakon.

Like everybody else, she'd been infatuated with the charming Prince. Tales had been told of his fight with his royal family, of his escapades with women from all over the world, the reckless car races and high-adrenaline sports he engaged in. She'd always been shy when it came to men, wary and reserved of slick charmers like him.

Didn't mean she hadn't mooned over him from a distance. The raw, pulse-pounding energy, the sheer masculinity of him had always made Nikandros ir-resistible.

Surrounded by A-list actresses and svelte models, he'd barely noticed her. There had been a freedom in being beneath his notice that had left her to indulge in girlish fantasies about him. Once Brian had asked her out—solid, reliable Brian—she'd given the unreachable Prince no more thought.

The reliable, hardworking man she'd fallen in love with had almost instantly disappeared the moment his soccer career had taken off. With each new contract, big endorsements and friendships with jet-setters like Nikandros, the Brian she had married had gone away, never to return.

And yet, Nikandros had always been present, like a specter in the background, always with a new woman on his arm, a new investment venture in hand.

His friendship with Brian had been the stuff of legends but she'd never made it into his exclusive circle. And the more death-defying stunts he'd taken on, the more Brian had wanted to be Nikandros, without success.

Whether genetics or blood or whatever the hell it was that made him, Mia had known no other man could be even remotely like Nikandros Drakos. A fact, when she'd pointed it out, Brian had resented like hell.

Through the years, through it all, it seemed Nikandros's and her mutual resentment had only thrived.

Slowly, she turned toward him. "I have had a long day, in my defense."

He considered her warily. Given that she *had* been

thrown under the bus by the media, he looked like the one who'd received the biggest, most humiliating news of his life.

Was Brian's betrayal truly that much of a shock to him?

"You should not be alone over the next few days. Brian would want—"

"Brian apparently wanted a lot of things I couldn't provide, Your Highness."

His usually languid mouth tightened. "Do not refer to me as such."

"But that is the correct way to address the scion of the ruling family of Drakon, yes? Now I understand the fits your aide was having when I got into your car. The last thing you need is for me to drag you into this media circus."

"Someone should look after you—"

"I've been looking after myself for a long time."

"Would your family not welcome you because of these…disgusting stories that the media has concocted?"

"Stories?" She tasted the bitterness in her mouth like it was a tangible thing. "If only I could borrow some of that delusion, I'd be able to sleep tonight."

Mouth flat, he leveled a dark look at her. "You could give Brian…his memory…a moment's benefit of doubt. You owe him that much. At least now."

At least now…" she repeated blankly. Slowly, the meaning of his accusation filtered in. "At least now when I didn't bother when he was alive, you mean?" Emotion balled up in her tummy and rose, finding a target for her fury. "Explain yourself, Your Highness," she said, encasing herself in steel.

Something glinted in those ice-blue eyes before that cool, icy reserve slid into place again. "Not the place or the time."

"Since I don't foresee a time or place when I want to see you again or have this conversation, please, *indulge me* with your summation of my marriage. The whole world's doing it. You may as well put in your verdict too. Especially because your friend's not here to defend himself."

He didn't look like the smooth, charming Prince that had longer relationships with his cars than his girlfriends, a man who was supposed to not give a fig about his family, or the fallout with his aging father, or his duty to his country—a man who only reveled in devilish pursuits of pleasure and sport.

The tight cast of his jawline, the way he gripped the steering wheel—she sensed that same swirling emotion in him that was within her too. "You're angry and hurt. And this is a conversation that I never meant to have."

For three years, she'd seen her marriage wither away inch by inch, mere months after tying the knot. For a year, she had battled the guilt of Brian's death. And today, just when she had begun to pick up the pieces of her life, it was all back in pieces at her feet. "You should have never implied that you did."

He turned toward her then, and the impact of his attention hit Mia like a punch. White shirt contrasting against the dark tone of his skin, he looked like a pagan god in the dark interior. A virile, pagan god, no less.

"I'm not offering excuses for what Brian did, if this is all true."

"Blind loyalty to your fellow macho man and blame for the woman—how pedestrian you are for all your blue blood, Your Highness."

A flare of anger in his blue eyes. "All I know is that he…he was crazy about you. He drove himself nuts wanting to fix your marriage but you froze him out. He was not the one who wanted to walk away from the marriage. Does that count for nothing?"

So he'd known that she'd asked Brian for a divorce. She hated how defensive she sounded yet she couldn't stop the words. "Words of love, promises of devotion are cheap. Actions speak much louder.

"From the moment his career took off, he changed. From the moment he entered your exalted circle, the moment he chose to emulate you and your death-defying stunts…he was lost to me."

The confusion she felt reflected in her voice. For three years, in the trenches of training and being un-contracted and poor, Brian had chased her with promises of forever and words of such deep affection, only to disappear the moment success had come calling.

"He chose to alienate me. He chose to get behind the wheel of that blasted car of yours and drive even though he was drunk."

"Mia, I'm—"

"And you…you've never even had a girlfriend. You change models and actresses on your arm as if they were an accessory. How dare you judge me for wanting to give up on a toxic relationship. I've had enough of you and your stinking opinions."

"Mia—"

She grappled for the handle of the door, the fierce knot of emotion rising from her chest to her throat. *Damned man and his damned car!* She felt the warmth of him caress her skin before she realized he had leaned over her to reach for the handle. Pure lean muscle grazed her heaving chest.

Her eyes closed; the whispers of her breath were like a drumbeat in her ears. Her lower belly felt molten, her entire body thrumming with tension. She willed her body to quiet down, to lose this painful awareness of his breath and breadth, of his compelling masculinity. Frustration to guilt to such deep want that it buckled her knees, she seesawed on emotions.

Finally, the handle clicked and she almost fell out.

There was a part of her that told her she was being irrational, that she couldn't just walk away from him in the dead of night. That his opinion, far from what she'd claimed, was mattering too much. But she couldn't grasp control over herself.

Had Brian told Nikandros everything? How Mia had stopped wanting to be near Brian, about how hard she'd found it to be touched by him once she'd learned of his first indiscretion?

Her trembling legs barely straightened when she heard him join her out on the dark road. Broad shoulders covered her. "You're being ridiculous, Mia."

The handle of the car pressed into her spine as she

tried to melt into the door. Anything to avoid the scent of him from entrenching deep inside her. Anything to stifle the overriding need to fall apart in his arms. "Go away."

He stretched his arms wide, jet-black hair falling forward onto his forehead. "I should not have spoken of Brian. Not tonight. Not when you're dealing with—"

She poked him in the chest, vibrating from the force of her fury. "You've no right to talk about our relationship, now or ever. And if that was an apology, then it stinks."

He caught hold of her wrist and crouched closer, his tall, lean body her entire world. Her belly dipped as he clasped her jaw, raising her chin to meet his gaze. "I've never apologized to a woman in my life. Except my *maman*."

He said *maman* with a French accent, a lilt to it. Like caramel over dark chocolate. "Then I'm shocked at the number of women willing to put up with you, Your Highness."

"Get back into the car. You can spend the entire night telling me how much I stink."

"Why are you being kind to me all of a sudden?"

He blanched, as if he hadn't realized it himself. The gleam of his blue eyes was mesmerizing in the moonlight. "I'm not an unkind man usually. I stayed back after that debacle at the press conference because I thought you…might need a friend." He pushed a hand through his hair, a rough exhale leaving his mouth. "But like every other time… I lost track of what I intended." His languid mouth curved in self-deprecation that made shock swirl through Mia. "Stay at my penthouse until this furor about Brian calms."

"No." Under the same roof with this man, and her emotions in a riot... A shiver snaked up her spine. "Thanks for the offer, but I... I need peace and quiet. Not Mr. Judgy looking down his nose at me when he knows zilch about relationships."

"You know a lot about my relationships. Or the lack of."

Her skin heated up, and she desperately prayed he couldn't see it. "You're not exactly known for your distance with the media. No wonder your poor aide looked like he had the worst job in the world." She ran a hand over her nape, exhaustion slowly creeping in. "I just want to go home."

"The press will be swarming there. My apartment has twenty-four-hour security and is a fortress against the media. You will be safe there."

The thought of the media shoving their cameras in her face, those salacious details of Brian's affairs—Mia sank back against the cold metal.

Hiding away in the Daredevil Prince's lair seemed like salvation.

"Admit it, you're tempted. This is not a situation either of us wants, but it was clear that I couldn't leave you there."

"Why were you at the press conference in the first place?"

After almost a year, her agent had convinced Mia that her fans needed closure, that she should announce her retirement from soccer publicly. Any contractual ties she'd had with Nik's team had been severed months ago when she'd learned that the third injury she'd sustained would damage her knee irrevocably if she continued to play.

At least, her everyday life hadn't been affected.

With that devastating blow and Brian's accident, her life had been on a downward spiral. The announcement at the press conference—it was to be a new start. Only she'd been ambushed by the press about Brian's affairs.

And Nikandros had been there.

Sweat beaded her brow. That nauseous feeling returned with a vengeance. "Did you know the news about Brian's affairs? Why didn't you warn me?" Her fingers bunched in his shirt, renewed betrayal coursing through her. "Or did you decide I deserved to be humiliated and turned into a spectacle for my alleged sins against Brian?"

His fingers clamped over her arms, the warmth from his body teasing her awake in more ways than one. "I did not know what was going to come out. Mia, I did not know what he…was doing with all those women. I… If nothing else, I would have told him he had a problem."

"Somehow I doubt that the vows of marriage would mean anything to a serial womanizer like you."

His chin drew back. "Who is drawing conclusions now?"

His eyes were hard, flat, his fingers tightening over her arms. He tensed, and then slowly the breath he'd been holding pushed out. She'd hurt him?

It was the most nonsensical thought on the most bizarre night of her life.

But then, the man she'd thought him to be would have never offered help tonight. He wouldn't have even looked at her twice, especially since it was obvious that he'd made up his mind that she had driven Brian away.

But Nikandros had never pretended a friendship or even an acquaintance. Among Brian's friends, he'd always maintained a polite, even wary, distance from her. As if she'd contaminate his pedigree if he got too close.

"Then why were you there? You sold the women's team, I know. They said you were leaving Florida. Maybe even the States. You dumped your latest girl-friend." She rattled off everything she had gathered about him from social media, a habit she hadn't quite kicked from when he'd first appeared on the scene.

"You had to know… Don't lie to me, Nikandros. God, please, no more lies."

Mia closed her eyes. It made her face the one thing she'd been trying to deny—that something inside her had sparked into life tonight, inside the car. Because of the Daredevil Prince.

The sense of him around her amplified a thousand times. The scent of him—dark and delicious and so fundamentally different from her own, clung to her nostrils.

So when he spoke, when his breath feathered over her skin, when his hands descended on her shoulders and pulled her into his body, when the strength and heat of him teased her into a desperate, deep longing, she drowned in the sensations.

She felt his powerful body shudder around her, felt his sharp inhale as he buried his nose in her hair, felt the raw, shameful urge to press her body into his, vibrating through her like a quake.

"I came because I needed to say goodbye."

A brittle laugh escaped her. "I don't believe you. You've never even considered me a friend. You couldn't stomach the idea of Brian marrying me. You—"

He pushed her away from him with a contained sort of violence that was far more terrifying than the way Brian used to lash out at her. Roughly, he pushed his hair back, his mouth curled into that familiar curve. "I couldn't stomach the idea of him with you because... I wanted you for myself.

"From that first moment when you came onto that field like a streak of lightning all those years ago, your joy on the field, your love of the game... I wanted all of that for myself."

Falling back a step, Mia stared. "What?"

The debacle of her marriage, the horrible truth of Brian's affairs, diluted as he spoke with a glittering challenge. "When he married you, I thought it would be done. That this infatuation with you...would die. All these years, I hated you for freezing him out, told myself I was lucky.

"Nothing helped.

"I came tonight because...even now, even after he's gone, I can't seem to stop.

"Stop thinking about you. Stop wanting you." Gripping her arms, he pulled her toward him until their faces were mere inches from each other. The gleam of his

blue eyes—Mia had never seen anything so beautiful.
"I came because I needed to say goodbye to a decade-
old obsession. To this madness.

   "Is that honest enough for you, Mia?"

CHAPTER TWO

DROPLETS OF WATER dripped from the ends of her still-wet hair, dampening the thin cotton of the oversize T-shirt that fell to her thighs. Shivering, Mia twisted the damp ends with her palm and squeezed the water onto the towel. She rubbed her hair one more time and threw the towel in the hamper.

Drying her hair seemed to need more energy than she had. Which was funny because she had just swum for an hour, running away as if from the very devil.

I wanted you for myself...

For hours on end, she found herself going back over every interaction they had had over the years, and like he said, God, they'd known each other for a decade. So many memories to sift through, so many interactions that she now viewed afresh.

How she wished she could cling to disbelief, to the outrageous hope that he had said that because he'd felt sorry for her. But the fire in his eyes—as if she were the next challenge he was contemplating.

She had no idea how she'd turned away from him and returned to the car, or what she'd even said when he'd brought her here. When he'd pointed it out, she'd fled into a bedroom and then, like clockwork, to the pool when it had struck midnight.

The corridor stretched now into the endless marble-floored open lounge with incredible views of Biscayne Bay's spectacular skyline on one side and Miami Beach on the other side. Tall palm trees and beach views told Mia she was in Miami and yet a world apart.

She wandered the penthouse, far too wired after the disastrous day she'd had.

There was a custom wine cellar, outdoor terrace, an indoor pool and an outdoor infinity pool, and four hot tubs with a bath deck overlooking the spectacular Brickell skyline.

Her feet sank deep into thick dark carpet as she walked into the media room. Colorful images moved soundlessly on the huge screen, and cast flashes of lightning into the vast, dome-like theater.

It was a recording of one of her own games—the championship game from three years ago when her team had won the World Cup.

A deep, shuddering ache went through her.

Heart steadily climbing, she found Nikandros seated on a step in the aisle. Arms leaning on his knees, his T-shirt highlighted the fluid line of his spine. Jet-black hair glinted with wetness every time the pictures moved on the giant screen. A half-empty, or rather a half-finished, bottle stood precariously on the carpet next to him, the liquid gleaming gold in it.

As if on cue came her powerful kick from the left field and the ball zoomed toward the net and past the flailing hands of the goalkeeper. The sound was on Mute, yet the applause roared in Mia's ears as if she were standing there on the field, the Spanish sun kissing her face.

The camera zoomed on her, sweaty and delirious with joy, her grin splitting her mouth into a wide curve.

A spark of joy lit up within Mia now, a quiet jolt as if she were being kicked back into life. On the screen, she did the victory lap around the perimeter of the ground and then that stupidly ridiculous dance, shaking her bum...

And the screen stilled on that image.

Nikandros was watching the game with an intensity that spoke of madness, obsession. It didn't matter that the Prince was known to be a hard-core fan of the sport, that it was the game that could have arrested his attention.

But no, he was watching her.

She walked down the few steps, heart pounding in her chest. "Turn off the game."

His body bent at an angle, he looked up. Long lashes cast crescent shadows on his cheekbones. But even those envy-inducing lashes couldn't hide the thorough way he stared at her, all the way from her wet hair to her bare feet. That same devilish half-amusement lingered around his mouth. "Don't tell me it's another eccentricity of yours, not watching yourself play?"

"Another one?"

"The midnight swim?" he added, gaze focused on the wet ends of her hair. "The isolation before a big game?"

Mia shrugged, the knowledge of how keenly he was

aware of her every eccentricity touching a fragile, buried part of her. His interest in her soccer career, *in her*,
was extremely addictive. And was going straight to her
head and other parts. "Only in the last few months have
I been able to accept that I'll never play again." She
looked up at the screen, an ache that never went away
settling deep into her. "That part of my life is over."

Up the steps and into the corridor she went, something uncoiling within her.

Something had changed tonight, even in the past
few minutes maybe—a line had been crossed, a line
between existing and living. The numbness that had
descended on her seemed to crack. A steely grip on
her arm halted her.

"I did not realize—" a restless kind of energy seemed
to radiate from him and it touched Mia like a spark to
dry tinder "—what you have gone through this past
year."

Her back to him, she pressed her forehead against
the wall, unable to catch her breath. Every inch of her
trembled from the small contact, every muscle locked
painfully against the impulse that was coursing through
her. "I hate it when you put it like that," she said into the
wall. "Like I was a victim. Of fate first, and then Brian.
I find this…that feeling unbearable. As if nothing was
in my control.

"For a year, I wallowed in that self-pity. With
Brian's affairs coming out—" a bitter laugh escaped
her "—strangely, I seem to have found myself again. I
refuse to be still anymore, refuse to be a victim."

The grip released on her arm. Now his fingers teased

her skin with soft strokes. "You astound me, Mia." His words were deep and low, with a longing that resonated with her own.

But he still didn't make a move on her.

Mia was terrified that he would and desolate that he wouldn't.

"I'm grateful that you were there today, Nikandros," she said, uncaring at this point that her voice betrayed her. "I didn't realize until now how much I needed a... familiar face."

Barely had her breath settled when she felt his hands slide to her shoulders. Her front was pressed against the wall, and at her back, he was a wall of warmth and want. With gentleness that undid her, he pushed her hair to the front and kneaded the hard knots on her shoulders.

His thumbs traced the sensitive skin at her nape. Breathing became a shallow exercise, a cavern of longing opening up within her. And then, just like that, he released her. "I will say good-night...and good-bye then."

She turned around fast.

Dark stubble gave him a grungy, roguish look. His swarthy skin, as always, contrasted with the glittering blue of his eyes, making the man knee-meltingly gorgeous. Blue shadows cradled his eyes. He looked different somehow.

Charm and looks had been a common enough combination in some of the male athletes Mia had known in her career. But all of it was blunted in Nikandros's case. As if they were nothing but surface traits.

It was the vitality that clung to his very pores, the

sheer virility of a man who pitted himself against the extremes of nature and won, that made every cell in her ping with awareness.

The word *good-bye* sat like a boulder on her chest. She wasn't prepared to say it. Not yet. "Where are you going?" she finally asked, carefully keeping her eyes away from the languid line of his mouth.

A self-deprecating smile carved a dimple in one cheek but left his eyes still far too intent on her. "To Drakon."

That Nikandros had turned his back on his royal family years ago—it was a little gold nugget the media recycled every few months. With his daredevil stunts and extreme sport enthusiast career, Nikandros regularly courted the media, and like faithful little dogs, they went digging every single time. No one, however, knew the cause of the falling-out.

"You're returning to your country?"

"For a visit, at least. My father's dementia has become public knowledge. The Crown Prince has summoned me. My sister and my mother, even though she divorced my father a while ago, think my brother needs me. Desperately, according to them. Although I can't imagine Andreas would know desperation if it smacked him in the face."

"How long have you been away?"

"A decade, maybe." The casual indifference couldn't belie the torment in his eyes. "This is the first time my brother has sought me out."

Clearly, he hadn't been expecting that. "I'm sorry, Nikandros," she finally said, sensing the ache in him.

He bent so suddenly that her breath whooshed out. One hard muscled thigh grazed the side of her legs, leaving her quaking. "Pity is not something I could tolerate."

"Did Brian's death make you feel sorry for me?" she countered. "Make you change your judgment of me?"

"No," he said without missing a beat.

"Honesty, honesty, my hide for honesty," she quipped in a singsong voice, giving in to the abrupt, insane urge to laugh.

Arms locking on either side of her head, he smiled. It touched his eyes then, which were like the sky on a summer afternoon. Time seemed to fly away, seconds turning to minutes and she felt the most insane urge to stop it. To grab it with both hands and hold on to this moment. "When do you leave?"

"Tomorrow morning."

That sinking feeling in her stomach returned. "I hope whatever it is that caused distance between your father and you…you're able to sort it out."

He plucked her hand from her side where she had fisted it tight. Tingles spread up her arm as he traced the half-moons left in her palm by her nails. "You and I both know that that's not possible. That nothing can make the distances carved over years lesser.

"I wish I could tell Andreas that I don't give a damn about our father or him or Drakon—" tension emanated from every inch of him "—but I find I can't."

Just when she thought she knew him, he said something like that. There was grief in his eyes, even pain. She didn't want to learn the cause of that grief; she couldn't ask why he'd walked away from his destiny when it was clear his family meant something to him.

"Apparently, I'm a pushover." An edgy grin, then laced with self-mockery.

"Or you have a serious case of hero complex," she said, wanting to make him truly smile. Even with his contempt for her, he'd stayed at the press conference, hadn't he? Thrill chaser or not, apparently Nikandros had a sense of responsibility.

"Families are never without complications," she offered. "But if there's a chance to say goodbye to him, you should take it."

"Are you estranged from your family too?"

She shrugged, not quite meeting his eyes. There was no point in dwelling on each other's past when, come tomorrow, they would never see each other again.

The inescapable fact was that tonight he seemed to need her just as much she did him—that bolstered her courage.

Soft strokes on her palms, to her wrists and above, all the way to the sensitive skin of her elbow. And back down. Every nerve tautened like the strings of an instrument.

Mesmerized, Mia couldn't lift her gaze from the sight of his long fingers on her skin. Those long fingers everywhere on her bare skin, stroking and caressing—she wanted to burrow into his warmth. "I don't want to say good-night yet."

He tensed. "If it's a shoulder you want to cry on, keep looking." A thread of anger touched his tone. "There's a line between challenging oneself and tormenting one-self and I've already crossed it."

Words came and fell away from her lips, desperate and hard. For the life of her, she couldn't put her want into words. How had he so cavalierly told her that she'd been an obsession he'd carried around for so many years? How hadn't he felt vulnerable?

Or was it strength to go after what one wanted?

Bracing herself on his shoulders, she pulled herself up and pressed her mouth to the corner of his. Stubble scraped her lips, sending sparks of rough sensation all over. His breath fell loudly in the silence. Under her questing hands, the muscles of his shoulders were like steel spikes.

Heart threatening to explode in her chest, Mia kissed the defined line of his jaw.

Another featherlight kiss over his cheek. One more at the corner of his mouth.

Icy blue eyes darkened to the color of a stormy sky as he looked into hers. Long fingers tightened against her scalp. He'd push her away, and she couldn't allow that.

Trembling from head to toe, she pressed her mouth flush against his. Jerked at the jolt of heat that coiled and uncoiled in corners of her body she'd forgotten existed.

Whiskey and heat—he tasted of sin, of deep desires she'd never indulged in.

She hadn't kissed a man in a long time, but this, it felt natural, almost inevitable since the moment she'd seen him stand amidst that teeming crowd.

Keeping her gaze open with a boldness she hadn't known she had, she traced his lower lip with her tongue.

Grasped the cushiony softness of it with her teeth and tugged at it. The moment she ventured inside his mouth, the tenor of the kiss changed.

It was as if an earthquake had rocked the world beneath her feet.

Wide shoulders and hard muscles, he slammed her into him, and she was drowning. He kicked her feet apart, his hard thigh shoving between her own. His tongue tangled with hers, in and out, sending such stabs of relentless heat through her that she retreated, breathless and scared.

A hand curled around her nape while another gripped her hip tight and pulled her hard against his rock-hard body. "Don't be scared of this, *Mia mou*."

Any little breath of air she had in her lungs punched out. The hard column of his thigh pressed against her core, rubbing sensitive nerves. Mia cried out, her knees jelly. His mouth devoured her as if she were much-needed air, as if he would drown without her.

It was a salve over the wounds that had dug deep during her marriage. She sank into his touch, energized by the possessiveness of it.

"Damn it, I hoped I'd be proved wrong." He almost sounded angry, his gaze a blue fire. "I thought I'd built you up, this attraction up into something more than it was."

Whatever little niggles Mia's painfully developed cautious nature threw at her dissolved at the potent need swirling in his strong face. He was right. This fire between them burned hotter and brighter the more they touched each other. It didn't matter why she was attracted to him, or why she wanted to feel the power of his honed body over hers.

She just did.

She sank her fingers into his hair, caressing the thick black locks, carving the strong lines of his face into memory when he picked her up and started walking.

His bedroom was three times the size of hers, with French doors opening out into an incredible view of the sea. Dark gray curtains and a huge plasma TV opposite the massive bed were the only belongings in the room.

Swallowing, Mia forced herself to look at the bed. The same dark gray sheets covered the sleek, contemporary bed. The image of Nik and she tangled in those sheets sent heat rushing to her face.

"You are scared."

She tilted up her face to see Nikandros unbutton his shirt and slide it off his wide shoulders. The insecurities brought on by the bed misted away at the sight of his broad chest. Liquid longing coursed through her at the defined contours and the sleek, tight flesh of his muscles.

"I have never…" The words died an instant death at the dark scowl on his face. "I'm not scared," she said, tilting her chin up.

Lethal challenge glinted in his eyes. "Prove it to me."

"How?"

"I took off my shirt. Now it's your turn."

She moved toward the bed and pulled off the duvet when she heard his sharp *No*.

"What?" she said, irritably.

She'd kept to her fitness routine almost maniacally

this past year, but the idea of being wanted by him would drive any woman to doubts.

"Here, Mia. In front of me."

"You've too many demands," she said, greedily taking in the bands of muscle in his abdomen. She licked her lips, imagining running her tongue over those ridged bands.

"I'm a demanding man. You will not hide from me or from yourself, *pethi mou*. I'm aware that you're jumping into this because we will never see each other again.

"But this night, this is ours. I have had ten years to imagine this moment. We're going to do this very, *very* thoroughly, and in full light.

"So, come, Mia. Let me see you."

Like a chastised student called to the front of the class, she dutifully moved back to the center of the room. Unbidden, snarky comments from Brian, always in this context, rushed into her head. Remembered frustration, with herself and him, propelled Mia forward. It was time to learn the truth.

"Two more steps," Nikandros commanded.

"You're enjoying this far too much," she complained, her eyes still glued to his bare chest.

He laughed. "I believe that is what we're supposed to do with each other—enjoy."

She came to stand a foot from him. And stiffened. Silvery moonlight filled the spot where she stood now. He would see every inch of her skin.

"You owe me a discarded T-shirt."

With fingers trembling violently, Mia rolled the edges of her T-shirt and pulled it off. The breeze from the sea was a soft caress against her heated skin. She threw the tee at him, her knees locked.

His gaze moved over her breasts, barely covered in her white lace bra. Her nipples became tight points, pushing against the flimsy fabric. The dark desire in those eyes gave her the courage she needed. She didn't wait to be commanded again. With one hand behind her back, she undid the hook and shrugged off the bra.

A gravelly whisper fell from his mouth. She'd have given anything to understand if her body pleased him.

"Come closer." His voice was a silken rasp over her naked skin. Panting breaths, his and hers, filled the velvety night. "*Christos*, Mia, do not argue."

"You owe me a piece of clothing, Prince," she demanded, lifting her chin.

With a casual movement of his hands, he unbuttoned his trousers and boxers, and stepped out of them.

He was huge, thick, jutting out and up toward his abdomen. Christ, he was bigger than she had ever imagined.

"All you have to do is ask, Mia, and you will have it," he purred, eating away the distance between them with one long stride. Mia realized that she had her panties on only when she felt a rush of wetness seep through the cotton fabric. She had never been this aroused even when… No, he was not allowed here, in this room, tonight.

It was just this gorgeous man and her tonight. One night.

Hands on her shoulders, Nikandros pulled her close and took her mouth in a kiss that sent rivulets of pleasure up and down her body. Calluses from the pads of his fingers scraped her skin, the difference in the texture teasing out responses like she had never known. He devoured her mouth—stroked her lips with his tongue and licked into her mouth as if he would leave no inch of her untouched.

Knuckles played over her back, digging and testing, up and down, side to side, as if she were his favorite instrument. Toes digging into the cold marble, Mia sank into his kiss. The graze of her breasts, nipples distended painfully, against his velvety smooth and hard chest sent their mingled groans out into the air.

The rub of her thighs was pure torture. Her body had always been her instrument—honed lethally with focus and determination for over ten years. And it had served her well in her career.

But now, it was totally out of control. The more Nikandros gave her, the more it craved, pulsing with longing.

With a deep groan, he lifted her off the floor until she was almost plastered to his hard body shoulder to shoulder, abdomen to abdomen. The press of his shaft against her belly seared Mia. The ache at the apex of her thighs grew as he rubbed the thickness against her belly, his hips thrusting against her.

She had no idea when he had divested her of her panties. Only when his long fingers dug into the curves of her buttocks did she realize that they were gone. Plundering her mouth, and then trailing wet, thorough kisses over her neck, he shifted her until his hip bone opened her up scandalously.

Mia sobbed, the friction opening her sex making her mindless with need. "Please, Nikandros…" she whimpered, past fear and inhibitions. Rubbing the aching folds of her sex against his bare hip wantonly.

He seated her on the high bed and stared at her breasts with an unholy gleam. She'd always been a natural athlete, her body more lean muscle than softness. Her breasts were on the smaller side too.

And yet, when Nikandros lifted them in his hands and kissed the voluptuous valley between, all the while muttering in Greek, Mia felt like the sexiest woman on earth.

When he lifted the dark, knotted nipple to his mouth and licked it, she arched her body toward him with a needy groan. He continued to lick and stroke the nipple until it was wet and so painfully sensitized that each ministration of his sent a twang of pleasure straight through to her sex. "I can't bear it," she whispered, her breath panting in and out of her like a whistle.

Release hovered on the edge of her consciousness, taunting and teasing, twined with this gorgeous man.

"But I have only just gotten started," he whispered, meeting her eyes. The devilish glint in them made Mia tremble all over. Still holding her gaze, he opened his mouth and closed it over her nipple. And did something that Mia had never imagined could be done between a man and a woman, something so wantonly glorious that a line of fire tingled down her spine.

Legs locked around his hips, Mia convulsed as he suckled on that nipple, his hands stroking every inch of her skin from her back to her buttocks. When he shifted his attention to the other nipple, she protested. Her mouth found his bicep. Damp and salty, he tasted like heaven when she licked him.

He kept up the strokes of his mouth over her nipple while his fingers separated the folds of her sex. When he pressed his thumb against the crest, Mia begged, "Please, now, Nik."

Instead, he took her mouth. The kiss was damp and hot, her erratic breathing slowly spiraling down to normal. And then he built her up again, until every muscle was taut and begging. And again. And again.

By penetrating her slick sex with two fingers.

By suckling on her nipple with such delirious intent that the peak hardened.

And every time she was near release, he pulled her back from it. Fists clenched on his muscled back, Mia sobbed his name over and over again, begging for relief.

Gentle fingers pushed her hair from her forehead, while he studied her with a slumbering gaze full of wicked fire. "What do you want?" she bit out hoarsely, lips swollen and stinging and her body trembling.

Stubble marks covered the swells of her breasts and her abdomen.

His tongue flicked out against her tight nipple, which made her core dampen even more. "To see you like this. Your brown eyes—always so wary and reserved, dark and dilated—your body, damp and flushed with need… you my slave in this bed."

"I hate you," she retorted, on principle, even as her body arched off the bed when he tongued her belly button.

"I know," he said with a wicked smile, and then he was rubbing that stubbly jaw against the tender skin of her thighs. Blue-black hair tickled the sensitive skin of her lower belly. Every pelvic muscle locked, tightened against his onslaught.

Digging her fingers in his shoulders, she said, "Nikandros—"

"Tut, tut, let me in, Mia," he said, firm hands pushing her thighs wide apart, until her slick flesh was all but open to his devouring gaze. His nostrils flared and Mia closed her eyes. Embarrassment and anticipation and soul-wrenching need—she was a cauldron of emotions.

The long muscles of her thighs convulsed when he bent his dark head and took a long lick of her damp folds.

Back arching off the bed, Mia pushed herself onto her elbows and dug her hands into his hair. Pleasure rode her lower belly hard as he kept up the strokes of his tongue. She writhed and moaned, but his arm on her belly locked her against the bed.

Again and again, he licked, driving her high, then easing up the pressure. The moment he sucked her tender flesh with his lips, Mia broke apart.

The wave of pleasure was so intense that she saw darkness and light. Deep, wrenching spasms of her muscles went on and on, while tears soaked her cheeks.

She barely caught her breath when he flipped her onto her stomach, and then pulled her up until she was on all fours. Her hair fell over Mia narrowing her view to the silvery sheets spread in front of her. She was still panting, echoes of her climax still twisting and turning deep inside her lower belly.

Only when his fingers, digging into her hips, pulled her back toward him did she realize her vulnerable position.

She tensed, the position alien and intrusive to her. How intimately he would see and know her like this...

He bent over her until his mouth reached the curve of her shoulder. Soft heat swirled through her pleasure-suffused nerves as he kissed her. His thick shaft wedged into the crease of her buttocks and Mia jerked at the strange, unraveling tingles in her sensitive tissues. Expletives filled the room, his breath hissing out of him.

"Do you not like it like this?" He sounded hoarse as if he were the one who'd already broken apart and been remade anew. Another kiss, this time with his teeth involved. The drag of his teeth against her skin made her breath rasp against the sheets.

The slide of his hot skin over hers, his breath caressing her neck, every inch of Mia felt carnal, as if her body had been made for only this purpose, only this man. Words were an impossibility.

"Ahh...and you think I'm gentleman enough to say fine."

She licked her lips, struggling to put her thoughts into words. "I don't know whether I will like it this way."

She instantly knew that he didn't like that answer. Whether he never liked hearing about his lovers' exes or particularly Brian, she had no idea. And she didn't care.

One long finger traced the line of her spine all the

way to the crease of her buttocks, teasing and taunting. A kiss landed on her left buttock and Mia blushed and burned in turns. Her arms ached, her body felt alien in the rivulets of sensations coursing through it.

She heard the whispered tear of a condom packet, and the sinuous slide of it over his shaft. Anticipation built like a balloon inside her and she felt him come up behind her.

Strong fingers drew a line of fire from her neck to her navel. "If it kills me, I'll make it good for you. Trust me?"

Breath on tenterhooks, Mia nodded.

"Say it, *pethi mou.*"

"I trust you, Nikandros. More than I've ever done anyone."

Hands on her hips, he entered her with one long stroke that set fire to her nerve endings. "*Christos*, you are tight." He shuddered around her, the hard muscles of his body locked tight, as if to stop himself from moving. "You needed more, Mia? Tell me you're okay."

First came an achy, alien sensation that threatened to buckle her legs under him. In this position, it felt like there was no part of her that Nikandros hadn't touched and claimed. "I'm…it feels…strange, but full, Nik."

He bent over her and kissed her damp skin, whispering endearments that sent a rush of tears to her eyes.

No, she didn't want tenderness from him. As if she were some fragile, breakable thing that he could not use the way he wanted. She wanted to be woman enough for him.

Slowly, she wriggled her hips back and forth, side

to side, getting used to his thick invasion. And with every movement, spirals of need swirled out from her sex. His breath slowed, deepened as she repeated the movements of her hips, and then pushed back in an inexperienced movement.

"Like that?" she said into the velvety dark depth of the night.

With a guttural curse, his fingers crawled up her back over her spine and into her hair. He held her so tightly that pain and pleasure infused together. Nik pulled out almost all the way, and then thrust back in so hard that Mia would have skidded across the bed if he wasn't holding her.

Pleasure so intense and so profound that she thought she might pass out radiated down her spine and speared her lower belly.

If not for tonight, if not for Nikandros, she'd have died never knowing that it could be like this. That pleasure could be so exquisite that one's soul could be remade from it. Her moans rose in pitch as Nikandros pounded into her, her name a guttural incantation on his lips, over and over. Mia didn't know how it was possible but her body was greedily racing toward another peak.

As if he knew her body better than she did, Nik pulled her close, fingers bruisingly tight on her hips. His thrusts became short and tight while one hand moved between her legs. "Come for me, Mia," he commanded, and then he gave her no choice but to follow him by tweaking her swollen clitoris between his fingers. Counterpoint to his hard thrusts.

Mia broke apart again with a soul-shattering cry.

Pleasure surrounded her in sharp, staccato bursts. He groaned as his thrusts lost the rhythm and finesse he had employed before and descended into purely animalistic movements.

This was what Mia wanted, what she needed. For this man, this gorgeous, powerful man who had given her a small part of herself back, for him to lose himself inside her. She wanted to steal away a part of him, even a tiny part, as he was doing to her.

The roar of his climax fell over her skin like some powerful magic returning and remaking her.

Tears coursing down her cheeks, Mia fell onto the bed and hid her face in the sheets. Every muscle in her body trembled. A sob fought to rise through her and she bit her lip to contain it. Limbs like rubber, she went willingly when he pulled her into the cradle of his arms. Words of gratitude, words of desperation rushed to her lips.

Her vision blurred, she looked down at them.

Moonlight played shadows over their twined naked limbs, damp, glistening skin and the rumpled sheets. Greedy even now, her gaze moved up one hair-roughened calf to the long, hard muscle of his thigh, the jut of his narrow hip bone. Carnal hunger and something else rang like a bell inside of her.

In gentle movements, he pushed back a lock of hair sticking to her damp forehead and pressed a tender kiss to her shoulder. "You're well?"

She could only nod. There was a glitter in his eyes, as if he too was shaken by the intensity of what they had shared. As if he too was...

No!

This was the Prince, a man who was so good in bed that women over the world chased him for one night... She couldn't make this moment any more than it was.

Her throat closed over words she couldn't say, a sudden weight on her chest. For the first time in months, grief and fury washed away, leaving a strange awareness of herself.

When he gathered her to him and breathed against her temple, she gave herself over to the beckoning hand of sleep that was taking over her mind, body and soul.

Nikandros Drakos was a fantasy come true, and in her case, he'd given her something immeasurable, indefinable.

But that's all he would ever be.

CHAPTER THREE

Six weeks later

"YOU'RE PREGNANT, MIA."

Her ob-gyn's soft declaration had kept ringing around in Mia's head all day as she set the high school soccer team through its drills as their new assistant coach.

Sheila, who had also known Mia since their mothers had dropped them off at the same elementary school, had held Mia's hand. "After everything you've been through this year, I… Mia, say something. This news could be a shock in itself but—"

"It's a shock, yes, but, oh…" Mia didn't know where the words had come from. She'd been alone for so long, but all she felt was overwhelming joy, a profound sense of anticipation in her chest. That night had been the beginning of a new chapter of her life and a child was the result. "I want this baby, Sheila. I…will love this baby."

That night back at the two-bedroom apartment she'd been allotted at the campus, Mia still couldn't stop smiling nor looking at her stomach in the mirror. Nor had her mind wavered even a little bit. But then, she'd always known her mind.

Accepting her new job, moving out of the apartment that Brian and she had shared—it had been the right move. Standing on the sidelines, watching young, ambitious players give their soul to soccer, it was fulfilling, yes, but life stretched ahead of her, a chasm of loneliness.

A baby would change everything, fill her days and nights. A baby she would love without conditions.

Even though there had been curiosity in her eyes, Sheila hadn't pressed Mia for details about who the father was.

The father. Mia fell back onto the couch in her living room with a soft plop.

Nikandros... Cold sweat gathered on her forehead.

This baby belonged to Nikandros too.

Not a day had gone by in six weeks that Mia hadn't thought about that night or him.

How could she escape it when every news channel was bleating on and on about the tiny principality of Drakon, the Mediterranean's Jewel, and the decline of its King Theos into madness, a fact that had been hidden from the media and its people for a long time? When every social media site covered the smallest movement of its Princes?

With a greed she couldn't curb, Mia had followed the news of the royal family. The media had been lambasting Nikandros yet again, for dereliction of duty and apparently not caring enough about the country.

Only Mia knew how much returning to Drakon had affected Nikandros, but even she found it easy to forget in the face of his merrymaking.

Not once had he answered the media's questions—would he stay in Drakon now and shoulder the responsibility of its people? Would he share his brother Crown Prince Andreas's burden?

Only deep silence from Nikandros. The pap had already caught him partying at a friend's nightclub, racing a dangerous curve in Drakon in a hell-on-wheels red Ferrari. The media then pronounced that the reckless Daredevil Prince Nikandros had reverted to form three days after the public announcement of his father's madness.

It was clear that the Daredevil Prince was not going to change his spots and settle down into responsibility. He had seemed so serious, so full of an unnamed pain to Mia, but now this, in front of his entire nation.

Had it all been just an act? Would he even acknowledge a child who had accidentally been conceived after a one-night stand as his?

Swallowing away the ache in her throat, the urge to share the news with him, Mia decided to wait to inform him.

At least, until she was strong enough to face Nikandros without weakening again. Until she was strong enough to face his reaction to their unborn child.

Nikandros stood on the ramparts of the King's Palace and stared out at the panoramic views offered of Drakon and the harbor. The smallish hill on which the eight-hundred-year-old palace stood had provided a strategic defense location from the numerous attacks through the centuries, from various regional and global powers who had always wanted to assimilate the small Mediterranean gem for their own.

But the House of Drakos—his ancestors, with this palace as their stronghold—had clung on, despite the attacks and defended the little jewel.

As a kid, stuck in the palace hospice during hot summers and mild, wet winters alike, Nikandros had loved the history of Drakon.

A dragon and its treasures and one band of fierce warriors, the stories had sustained him through a wretched, ill childhood. He'd inhaled the old volumes in the vast library, breathed in every arch, wall and wing that had been added to the King's Palace by each generation, making it impregnable. With no children to play with, he had weaved elaborate dreams picturing Andreas and himself as modern princes who would deliver Drakon from its various nemeses.

Crown Prince Andreas, his older brother, would command him, and Nikandros, his loyal knight, would jump to do his bidding.

"Why won't he visit me, Maman?" He'd relentlessly plagued his mother with the same question every time they had seen Andreas on TV, standing proudly by their father.

"You'll join him when you're feeling better, ma cherie,*"* his *maman* would say.

But Andreas had never had time for the attention-craving, mostly ill Nikandros. Nor had King Theos ever shown any interest in him beyond inquiring of the doctors if his spare was going to make it.

Not until Nikandros had turned nineteen and finally, against all medical predictions, seemed to have cast off the sickness that had plagued him all his life. And then, only then, had Theos entered Nikandros's life.

"I should have sent the guards to this terrace to look for you," came the deep voice of his brother, Crown Prince Andreas. A small smile flitted over Andreas's lips, as if this was one of those sweet memories that siblings shared. That is, if the siblings had come from a normal family and were not *the much-adored son and heir* of a little mad, power-obsessed King and *the spare* he had barely tolerated and known even less.

"I have no idea what you're talking about," Nik drawled in a careless voice, forcing himself to relax his tight grip on the stone wall.

"The nurses used to run over the palace looking for you, only to find you here amongst these ramparts, waving that rubber sword around with barely a stitch over your body. This was your favorite place," finished Andreas, coming to stand by Nik.

"How the hell would you know?" *When you barely ever saw me*, he didn't say.

"The study in my wing has a window that provides a perfect view of this very terrace. I would watch you brandish that rubber thing, fighting off imaginary enemies. If not the ramparts, it would be stables. Third choice, the kitchens." The wistfulness in his brother's voice cut Nikandros.

Thick silence descended over the terrace. Nik stared

at the gaunt hollows of his brother's face shadowed in the waning light of the sun.

Theos was slipping, had descended into the final stage of the dementia that had claimed him for the past few years. The sight of his once-proud and overbearing father with that crazed look in his eyes, and fragments of gibberish falling from his lips—it had shaken him deeply.

And yet it was the look in Andreas's eyes that rooted him to the spot.

Andreas had been dealing with his father's madness for years now, and the country's declining morale, and the power-hungry Crown Council.

Guilt twisted deep and low in Nik's gut. He'd known what was happening but had refused to come. "It is a little late to pretend we share a brotherly bond, Andreas."

The infuriatingly amenable expression did not budge from his brother's inscrutable eyes. He wished Andreas would throw a punch at him. Or call his actions despicable. But of course, his brother would never oblige.

He hadn't back then, when Nik had told Andreas what he had done with his precious fiancée, and he wouldn't now.

"Why did you return then, Nik? Did you finally feel pity for me? Or dare I hope that you have grown a sense of duty to your country?"

Damn Andreas for always knowing the right question to ask. Nik himself didn't know the answer to that question.

Had he done it because the sense of history, the heritage of Drakon that he had always yearned to be a part of when he had been a little boy, had sunk its claws into him again?

Or had he done it because leaving Drakon would mean facing that all the little things that had previously given him such pleasure still paled when he thought of one ex-soccer player?

"I promised *Maman* I would stick around for your coronation."

Andreas's mouth flattened. "The coronation is postponed."

Nik frowned. He knew that these past few years, behind the curtains, Andreas had run the show. So why was his brother, who'd been born and bred into the role of King, now postponing the coronation? "With Theos frothing at the mouth, Drakon needs you at the helm."

"So you do think about Drakon then."

"Why did you ask me to return? And the truth, Andreas."

Nik folded his hands, his stance clearly belligerent. But Andreas would never take the bait. He would never do something as emotional as get into a fight with his brother.

"I need you, Nikandros."

It was, apparently, a time for shocks. First Brian, then Mia, then his father and now Andreas.

Andreas sighed. "The Council has been getting more and more disturbed about my lack of marriage. With father's final decline fast approaching, it is now a matter of public and political concern owing to legal and international consequences. If I should die tomorrow suddenly, our treaty with our powerful neighbor becomes void and we could be annexed.

"The economy is on a nosedive and financial analyses do not show it recovering anytime soon."

"Then why didn't you marry that…*woman* and produce heirs by now?" Nik interrupted, bile rising even at the thought of her and what he'd done.

"If you had bothered to visit once or inquired after us, you'd have learned that I broke that engagement with Isabella as soon as you left."

"I've not heard a whisper of it."

Andreas shrugged. "Because it worked well for me and Isabella to let the world believe I was engaged to her for a long while. Her brother wanted it said that she'd walked away from the alliance. Rejected the Crown Prince of Drakon.

"I agreed."

"Father must have hated that."

"Father and I have learned to understand each other better," Andreas said cryptically.

"What I did then was—"

"I don't want to dwell in the past, Nikandros. It would not show either of us well, *ne*? The point is I need your help, in a hundred ways. And I believe you possess a far more giving nature than I do.

"I need father declared incompetent, to build Drakon's economy back up again and its morale, to stop the Crown Council from dictating my life."

Nikandros had heard from numerous sources of his own the unrest among the populace, the slow exodus of businesses to their competitive neighbor, of deals falling through and investors pulling out because Andreas would not announce the date of his engagement, much less the wedding.

Because Andreas would not bow to the Crown Council's demands, and he, Nikandros, had turned his back long ago on Drakon.

Which was why he'd stayed longer than he'd planned to, the challenge it presented to his business sense engaging his interest despite himself. The economy of Drakon was ripe for the taking. Tourism could be boosted, some of the old ways let go of... Much as he wanted to deny the knowledge, Nikandros understood perfectly what Andreas wanted and Drakon needed—fresh blood. "Then marry, Andreas."

"I will not rush into any alliance before weighing the long-term needs of Drakon. I have to appoint you the Hereditary Heir, Nik."

Nikandros had walked out on his family years ago, publicly declaring that he was renouncing his status as second in line to the throne.

But Andreas's words began to tug at a powerful desire he'd denied for so long. *Christos*, once he'd loved his homeland with everything he had. Walking away from it had almost destroyed him. It had also been his salvation because only away from his father's and Andreas's shadows had Nikandros come into his own.

Discovered himself.

"Once I produce heirs, you will be bypassed for the throne, if that's what worries you. But I need your business sense, Nikandros, your networking skills. Drakon needs you.

"I have some things to take care of," continued Andreas, staying calm as always. "An expedition to the North Pole, for example."

Nik laughed, this sound rolling out of him like an avalanche. "I do not believe that you want to go off on some expedition to the ends of the world. You don't have a drop of adventurous blood in you. Or a vein of fun either."

His words fell into the silence like harsh stones being pelted against a smooth marble floor. If there had ever been that zest for something more than duty in Andreas, their father had eradicated it. Snuffed it out. For more than twenty years, Theos had closeted his heir in the palace, training him to take over the principality, cutting off Andreas from kids of his age, any other pursuits, from Nikandros and Eleni, maybe from life itself.

"But that is exactly what I'm doing, Nik. Trying to lessen my burden without disastrous consequences."

"So you would have me be the prop that Theos wanted me to be?" taunted Nik.

"His reign is over, Nik. You and I are the future."

Nik had never come so close to being persuaded into the belief that he too had a part in his country's politics. But something inside him balked at trusting Andreas. At being amidst these walls where he'd always been the weakling, the runt. "I wish I could help, but no."

Frustration uncoiled in his brother's edgy movements. "Have you ever thought that maybe I do need you, Nikandros? That Camille and Eleni need you? That the populace of Drakon that gave you this privilege need you?"

"*Maman* chose you, her stepson, over me," he threw back at Andreas, shivering with that impotent rage. His mother had divorced Theos the minute Nikandros hadn't needed her anymore. And yet, she chose to live in Drakon, at one of Andreas's estates.

"Maybe because Camille knew I needed her more than you." The glimpse of helplessness in Andreas's eyes stunned Nik. "Are there more women to seduce? More dangerous expeditions to take on? Your new lover, Mia Rodriguez Morgan—"

"*Christos*! You've had your staff spying on me?"

There was not an ounce of guilt on Andreas's face. Any pain Nik had felt two minutes ago drained, leaving fury in its wake. "This is exactly why I left this bloody palace! To escape father's machinations and manipulations!

"And you want me to trust you?

"You're every inch his son, Andreas, from that ruthless will that will crush anyone in its wake, from the way you manipulate *Maman* and Eleni, to your blind devotion to Drakon.

"He has made you in his image—a monster puffed with privilege and power. And if you don't take care, you'll descend into that same madness, just like him!"

Like a rock, a giant boulder, very much like the one the palace had been built on ages and ages ago, Andreas didn't even flinch. He still had every ounce of his control, whereas Nik was barely holding on to his.

"What happens if she takes that story to the tabloids?"

"I've had lovers before. Mia's no different." She was no more than an obsession that had been satisfied.

She had to be. Even if the memory of that night never seemed too far from his mind. Or his body. Even if her innate sensuality that night was in direct contrast with some of the things Brian had carelessly said about her.

After all these weeks, Nik couldn't hide from the fact that his night with Mia had been more than fantastic sex. But he could no more pursue a relationship with Mia than he could become his brother's best friend.

Andreas was relentless. "It makes no difference to you then that the child she's carrying might be yours?"

A child? His child?

Ice curdled in his veins.

He grabbed the lapels of his brother's shirt and forced him close. And now, after he had shattered Nik's own world with as much subtlety as a hammer blow, shock reverberated in his brother's eyes. "You did not know."

"You are making this up. You'll do anything, tell any number of lies to get what you want."

While he stood like the same bloody castle that he was the lord of, against attacks and sieges through the ages, a little whiteness emerged around Andreas's mouth. "You made your anger and disgust for father and me known on every occasion, with every stunt you pulled, with every outrageous expedition you took on. And yet you carry on his tradition.

"You seduce women all over the world without thinking of consequences, and now you follow in his footsteps leaving your little bastards all over the place." Andreas turned away from him.

Nik's head spun around in dizzying circles. If not for

the shock, he'd have thought those violent dizzy spells from his childhood were back.

He hadn't figured out his own life yet, swinging from one adventure to the next, playing hide-and-seek with death again and again—and he had fathered a child?

A new life Mia and he had created that night...

He closed his eyes and let the inky darkness envelop him. The idea of walking away from this as he'd done with everything else in his whole life was a tempting notion.

His duty to Drakon, toward his family, lovers, girl-friends, careers—he'd made not settling into anything, walking away from everything, into an art form.

All he thrived on was the next challenge, the next horizon and not looking back.

He should do the same this time too.

The child would be better off. And he... His heart pounded in his chest as Nik sifted through his own tumultuous feelings, trying to grasp them before they slid away like water in a fist.

He didn't do commitment, he didn't do relationships. But still...

A family unit—and not the dysfunctional circus he'd been born into. *Christos*, it was what he'd wished for every Christmas when he'd been a kid.

Could this be his chance to carve a family that was just his own?

Knowing that a child he had created was somewhere in the world, unaware of his existence, not being a part of that child's life—it would be unbearable.

"I don't trust you. And I don't trust what I become

around you," he said, knowing that Andreas still stood there, waiting to see if Nikandros needed him.

It would have meant a lot in the distant past. He would have gone down on his knees for an affectionate word from his brother through the long years of loneliness.

But Nikandros had stopped needing any of them—Theos; or his mother; his sister, Eleni; or Andreas—a long time ago.

They had all, at one time or the other, chosen Andreas over Nikandros.

They had forced him to become this man, forced him to leave that childish naivete, that dreamer behind. They'd ripped off the blinders he'd worn as a boy.

"I'm making amends, Nikandros, for father and my own…actions. You belong in Drakon."

This was what Andreas had intended from the moment he had stepped onto the terrace seeking Nik. Reparations or not, Andreas was their father's son to the last cell.

But all Nik could think of right then was the idea of a child—his child—and the woman he shouldn't have tangled with at all.

CHAPTER FOUR

MIA HAD NO idea how it had happened. One minute, she was parking her Toyota under the covered lot, and the next, the media seemed to swarm her from all sides.

Sweat pooling down her back, she wondered if she should drive away, when she saw two tall, burly, plainly dressed men with wraparound shades create a subtle pathway from her car to the lobby.

Mia grabbed her handbag, pushed the car door open and hurried inside. She took the steps to her first floor apartment, her mind whirling. Those men—suddenly she knew whose men they were. Hands shaking, she rummaged through her bag for keys when the door to her apartment opened.

The intimidatingly wide, dark male who stood in the center of her living room made her heart pound dangerously.

Clad in a sky-blue polo shirt that made his eyes gleam and black jeans, was Nikandros. Mouth dry, she stared at him, the spacious open layout she loved about the lounge shrinking around him.

Shock gave way to something far more elemental as

questions pounded at her. *Had he been unable to stop thinking of that night too? Had he—*

The second their eyes locked, sensations that made her skin stretch tight over her muscles poured in. The hard weight of him inside her body, pulsing and thrusting, the deep clench of her core around him, the tremors that had breathed new life into her very veins...

Shying away from his penetrating stare, Mia went to the kitchen and poured herself a glass of water. Her back to him, she drained it. Her hand went to her abdomen. She hadn't imagined seeing him anytime soon. Didn't know the first thing she was going to say to him.

"I will stand here all day, Mia. Patience is one of the few virtues I possess." But the patience in his tone was exaggerated, only a thin veneer.

Taking a deep breath, she turned.

Sunlight from the little kitchen window fell in beams over his sharp, lean features. Jet-black hair a little long. The undone buttons on his T-shirt revealed bronzed skin stretched tight over defined pectorals. The solidly male strength of his thighs encased in black jeans—her insides quaked.

Stomach flip-flopping at the scent of his aftershave as he invaded the small space of the kitchen, she leaned against the counter for support. "What're you doing in my apartment?"

"I convinced the security guy in the little hut that I was a friend you'd appreciate seeing in the midst of that media jungle. He was more than happy to have the assistance from my guards."

"I might not be the Princess of some Mediterranean jewel but I've just as much right to my privacy."

He raised a brow, the cast of his features taut. She flushed, wishing she could keep her tone neutral. But seeing him turned her knees to jelly and jumbled up her emotions, and the animosity in her tone was her only defense. "And here I thought I'd be welcome again after such a warm reception the last time."

She moved away from that confining space and walked into the living room, hoping a little distance would even out her body's intense reactions. "That night—" a flush overtook her but she forced herself to say the words "—was a one-off. It didn't make friends of us, Nikandros."

Hands at the nape of his neck, he twisted it this way and that, while his gaze stripped her to the core. The movement stretched his T-shirt tight against his lean chest. "I'm glad there's no misunderstanding on that front."

Mia flinched at the sharp derision in his tone. "Why don't you tell me why you're here," she challenged, ignoring the fact that the longer she didn't bring up the news of her pregnancy, the messier things would be between them.

But his easy dismissal, when she hadn't been able to forget for a single minute of what they had shared, stung.

Long, powerful strides covered the distance that separated them until he caged her against the couch.

Blue eyes glittering, he seemed nothing like the man who had folded his huge body around hers in a gentle embrace that night. Nothing like the man who had jolted her into life after three long years. "The only reason those wolves outside didn't bombard you with questions about the pregnancy is because my aide manipulated them with the offer of a statement."

Her knees giving away from under her, Mia fell into the couch behind her. A block of chill ice seemed to radiate inside her despite the sweltering heat of the day.

Nikandros Drakos, Mia had forgotten, was a darling of the press.

For all his irresponsible, death-defying ways, he was charming, approachable, the most down-to-earth member of a royal family that was shrouded in secrecy. He had the media eating out of his hand most days.

"Is it mine?" The question reverberated in the sun-dappled silence.

She looked up, tension swirling around them thickly.

The wind chimes she'd tied outside rattled in the wind, the tinkling sound mocking her. This baby was supposed to be a new start for her. Without the complications of a man, without her own fears leaching away her chance at happiness.

"How did you know?" He'd been an ocean away, existing in a world different from hers.

"Christos, Mia, just tell me if it's mine."

What did he want? What would he do? Would he demand that she not tell anyone?

A man like Nikandros thrived on the next challenge, on the next conquest. The last thing he'd want was to be tied to a woman and a baby.

He sat down on the coffee table, once again locking

her against the small space with his long legs. Thighs that had straddled her in the most intimate way blocked her movement. Mia's breath stuttered in her throat. Jeez, she had to stop thinking of that night.

"If you're even considering lying, Mia—"

Her own temper flared as she met his accusing gaze. "Of course, the baby is yours. I hadn't been with a man in three and a half years before that night."

Deep grooves etched into his forehead; a stillness came over him. His gaze searched her face, and then a long breath left him in a shuddering exhale.

That simple exhale said everything he didn't. Mia looked down at the white knuckles in her lap. "I was going to tell you soon, once I processed it myself." His prolonged silence made her insides twist and she babbled on. "I mean, we used a condom. My cycle hasn't been regular since I stopped playing and the pill was messing with the pain medication after the injury and I didn't think much of it until…" Her face flamed as she realized what she'd blurted out. "It came as a shock," she added lamely.

"Not the third time."

"What?" She raised a confused gaze to him.

"I didn't use a condom that third time. At dawn. When I found your behind so neatly and tightly tucked up against my groin."

Mia closed her eyes, wanting to hide away from starting this thread. Instead, the memory of Nikandros coaxing her awake in the most raw, elemental way ever…

An expletive exploded from his mouth, snatching

Mia back into the now. "I've never been so irresponsible about—"

She covered his mouth with her hand, unwilling to hear him say that it had all been a mistake. That was one thing she couldn't bear to hear, whatever the consequences they were facing now. "I could've…reminded you."

Except she hadn't been capable of a single rational thought by then. Instead of letting her leave, he'd slept by her side the whole night, and the solid, comfortingly male warmth of him, the sheer feeling of being held like she was precious in those corded arms… Mia couldn't have moved if her life depended on it.

That night had been about more than fantastic sex. Yet, she couldn't share that with him. Not if she wanted to retain her sanity.

"I take responsibility for it. All of this. For that night and the consequence."

He raised that brow again, a derisive glint in his eyes. "Yes? For all of it? If I didn't have a vivid memory I think you would try to convince me that you seduced me against my wish." He sighed. "But we were both there."

"I mean it, Nikandros. I've made my decision and I—"

"I would be delighted if you'd share this decision with me."

His sarcasm stung. "I realized I'm ready to be a mother. I asked him, but Brian never…" The sudden tenseness of his posture made her swallow her next thought. Her ex's name had somehow become a dirty word between them. Yet, she felt the most insane urge to explain herself, to go over her disastrous marriage so that Nikandros would understand.

Absolutely insane—because Nikandros was not her future and Brian was her past.

"I will love this child, Nikandros, more than I've ever loved anyone else."

The flat line of his mouth seemed to go back to its natural shape. "We agree on something."

"What's that?"

"That a child should be loved irrespective of who they are or how they came to be."

Shock was too tame a word for what resonated through Mia. She'd been loved like that once, without conditions, without reservations. And when she'd lost it, something had forever frozen inside her.

The Daredevil of Drakon, it seemed, was as conventional as a man could be, in this.

"You should have contacted me immediately."

"You had a lot going on," she added defensively.

"The events in my life have nothing to do with your...with this."

"Your father's deteriorating health, Brian's death—they had everything to do with us. We don't even...like each other. We were not ourselves that night." Accusation she fought hard to keep out of her tone sneaked in anyway. "You went straight back to it all—the nightclubs, the car races. It seemed you had put that night thoroughly behind you. Moved on."

"From you, yes," he said, in a voice that could freeze her blood. "I was done with you. Whatever obsession I had with you was satisfied."

He walked to the French doors and looked down, leaving Mia reeling from that easy dismissal. Of course, what had she expected from a man who'd dated some of the most beautiful women in the world?

That he'd been unable to get that night out of his mind? That it had been special? It was telling what foolish hopes she'd harbored even when she didn't want this to go any further.

His lithe frame turned around, his gaze far-off. "This place is not safe for you anymore. Brian's affairs, his shadow, they haven't left you yet. You need to leave."

"I can't run away because of a few reporters."

He didn't even seem to hear her. "We'll leave for Drakon immediately. Pack what you can, the rest you can buy there."

Rushing to her feet, Mia wrapped her fingers around his forearm. "Wait, what? What are you talking about?"

The moment the pads of her fingers grazed the sinews of his forearms, heat swirled between them. He slowly pulled her hand away from him and dropped it.

But even that simple touch made memories of that night burst into the space between them.

Languorous mouth kissing her spine, a hand stroking between her thighs, waking her up with such sizzling heat—the moment was so vivid that a soft gasp slid out of Mia's mouth.

"You still want me." He said it so clinically that it cut through the desire, making her feel foolish. "That's a start, I suppose, if the worst had to happen."

"I don't want you," she breathed out, her protest pitiful in the face of her body's obvious response. "And this baby is not the worst that could have happened, not for me."

"Maybe not the child, but a relationship with one's dead friend's ex is hardly the auspicious start one hopes for. You wouldn't be the woman I'd have chosen to carry my child. Not when your history with him will always hang over our heads. Not when..." He bit away the words, a dark shadow in his eyes. "But then, I should've thought of that before I arrived at that blasted press conference.

"Poor impulse control has ever been the bane of my life."

"That history could be clarified," Mia bit out, struggling to sort through the grenade he'd thrown down, "if you do me the courtesy of letting me speak about Brian and me. But of course—" Only now did the first part of his derisive comment sink through. "What the hell do you mean, a relationship?"

"You didn't think I would ask if the child was mine, and then calmly walk away, did you?"

She stepped back from him, a cold sweat breaking out along her neck. "*It is* exactly what I expected of you from the moment I got the news." Exactly why she hadn't panicked about his role in all this. Which she definitely was now.

"It's your fault for thinking you know me, Mia," he said with a hardness in his eyes.

"I've followed your lifestyle for a decade now. You're nothing if not predictable. Women and thrills—you're a daredevil who likes to live on the edge, Nik. You can't fault me for thinking you'll run in the other direction when your one-night stand ends in an unexpected pregnancy."

Gut twisting, Mia tried to ward off the panic flooding through her veins. A relationship with Nikandros was the last thing she needed in her life.

So why wasn't he running?

Nikandros ran a hand though his hair, staring as color fled Mia's honeyed skin.

Why was he thinking of marriage when there were a hundred things already muddying their relationship? Was he being driven yet again by his impulses?

No answer came forward.

Except that he still wanted her. Beyond madness. *Still. Again.* As if wanting Mia was a part of his own makeup now.

And she wanted him, for all her protests. Nothing could hide the darkening pupils nor her stuttering breath every time he ventured close.

He'd looked up old girlfriends in Drakon just as an exercise and had felt nothing. Yet, even snarling at each other with Mia was more exciting than anything he'd felt in a long time.

Her eyes wide, her mouth trembling, she looked at him as if he were the only man in the world for her. As if she wanted nothing but for him to kiss her again.

He wanted to kiss the confusion away from her mouth, he wanted to forget the world outside—forget Andreas and Theos and bloody Drakon and lose himself in her again, to find that peace that had settled over him when he'd held her.

To chase that inexplicable connection he'd found with her.

This fiery need between them, it should've been a red flag even that night. They'd come together like an explosion that first time.

So he'd indulged, again and again. He'd pushed them both to the edge, desperate to lose himself, desperate to fix the emptiness he couldn't seem to outrun.

The consequences—nothing good had ever come from Nikandros indulging his emotions like that. Nothing but destruction came of him weakening and giving in to his impulses.

"Nik, listen to me. As long as we keep your…role in this quiet for now, I'll be fine. Once the baby comes and the furor has calmed down, we can discuss visitation rights. I'm glad you think the child's well-being is important."

"My role in this?" he taunted, his ire rising.

"I…will never come forward at a later time and demand anything. You cannot expect me to uproot my life and stay in Drakon while you continue…your reckless playboy lifestyle."

"You will have time to state your requirements of this marriage, as I shall tell you mine. There's no other choice but to make it work. My child will not be born a bastard."

The blood drained from her face, leaving the honey gold of her skin washed out. "What?"

"Whether now or years later, it will out that it is mine. If it's not your doctor, it will be your best friend. Or your landlord. Already, there has been a leak, yes?

And the world will call it another bastard from the House of Drakos. The media will hound it for the rest of its life.

"That is not acceptable. This child will be born in wedlock and inherit everything that is rightfully his or hers."

"You've lost your mind."

The more her panic rose, and she stood straight and stiff like a glass pane about to break, the more Nikandros's own resolve solidified. The restlessness that had clawed at him all these months, was this the answer?

He'd realized the daredevil lifestyle had begun to lose its glitter.

Was it time for a new direction in his life?

An attraction that defied all the usual conventions and a child on the way—was it enough to make a marriage?

It had to be. For he could never walk away from his own child. And this was not an impulse. Or a challenge. This was the only rational way forward. For both of them.

"No, I've never actually been this lucid before. We will marry as soon as possible."

Mia kept shaking her head and moving away from him, as if physical distance could push him out. "For one thing, I never want to marry again, and even if I did for some life-changing reason, I wouldn't marry a man like you."

"What the hell does that mean?" he bit out, forgetting his every tenet to keep this civil.

"You're not the sort of man a woman wants to tie

herself to in marriage, Nikandros. Your dangerous career, your death-defying stunts…your reputation with women—constancy and stability are not in your dictionary.

"I *will not* spend the rest of my life with a man like you."

This was the price of his obsession. The price of going too far. Of all the women in the world, it had to be his friend's ex, the one woman he should have kept away from, who was going to be his child's mother.

It was as if he'd gone for the worst sort of woman for him and invited her into his life. Damn it, why couldn't he just walk away? Why couldn't he make an arrangement like his father had done with his sister, Eleni?

To this day, Nikandros did not know what had attracted him to her that day on the field. But instead of pulling out that splinter, he had fed his obsession, let it dig deep into him for so long that he had no memory of a day when he hadn't wanted Mia.

She was a jagged thorn nestled far under his skin. A conquest he couldn't quite conquer. "This from the woman who looked me in the eye and told me to take her without question…"

Mia looked away, images of their moon-kissed bare limbs tangled in the sheets drenching her. Even now, when she could feel those shackles that terrified her pulling her to him, she couldn't regret her actions that night.

But letting Nikandros into her life—Nikandros, who pursued thrill after death-defying thrill as if his sanity depended on it; Nikandros, who walked away from his family in pursuit of that lifestyle—it would break her like nothing before.

Didn't he see that they would only bring out the worst in each other? That, in a few years, he'd resent her at best and hate her at worst?

She hardened her tone, despising him even more for what he was forcing her to say. "I, clearly, needed sex and you…you provided it."

Arctic frost would have nothing on the coldness of his blue eyes. "So all you needed was a stud? Any man would have done?"

"Maybe, I don't know." She brazened it out past the hard lump in her throat. "What I know is you… You're the most gorgeous, the most compelling man I've ever met. You taught me more about my body than I ever knew… But you're not marriage material, Nikandros.

"A mere two weeks after your accident at your latest stunt—scaling that mountain peak—you went back to that crazy lifestyle again.

"When you were in Drakon, I waited and watched, like the entire world did, to see what you'd do. If you'd settle down. If you'd own up to your duty…

"Not once did you tell the media that you'd stand by your brother now.

"You walk away from responsibility in your life. You risk your life again and again. And you want me to trust that you're interested in being a husband all of a sudden, that this child is not a novelty?

"I won't be locked in another marriage, with a man even worse than Brian."

"And the child? Have you decided that it doesn't need a father, either?"

"It definitely doesn't need a father who chases death-defying thrills as if it were an addiction. It does not need a father who's only going to break his or her heart in the end.

"Let's face it, Nikandros, you're no more equipped to be a father and a husband than you are to become the Prince that Drakon needs."

Tall and proud, his eyes flinty with a hardness she'd never seen in him, Nikandros stared at her. The seconds ticking by made the hair stand on her nape.

"I never planned to marry either. I never envisaged a marriage to a wife who'll remind me every day that she drove my friend to near madness, a wife who'll treat the father of her unborn child with little respect, as if he were nothing but a sperm donor.

"Not in a hundred years would I have chosen that life—filled with mistrust and contempt. *Christos*, I walked away from that life and made something of myself. But see, there is one thing where you went wrong in your estimation of my character, Mia.

"I have never walked away from the consequences of my actions. Neither will I now."

Fear rippled down Mia's spine. "You can't force me to go with you."

He opened the door and beckoned someone inside.

It was the short, squat man Mia had seen hovering around Nikandros's penthouse. The man looked at Mia and Nikandros, back and forth, as if he could sense the chill in the room despite the sweat beading on his bald head.

"Your Highness, the Crown Prince has—"

Nikandros interrupted the man without even looking at him. "On my signal, Stavros here will tell the press that the child you carry is mine. One word that you hooked up with your late husband's best friend and the press will hound you. Every wrong Brian committed against you will be forgotten when they learn that you shacked up with me and are now carrying my child."

"You're bluffing," Mia croaked, despite the icy chill in Nikandros's words. He looked like he was carved from the very mountains his country seemed to be full of. No cocky smile lingered around his mouth. No twinkle softened the coldness of his eyes. "You aren't that ruthless, to serve me up to them. That's not the Nikandros I know."

"Oh, *agapita*, but we've already established that you do not know me.

"I've been that ruthless once before. And even then, I surprised myself with how cruel I could be. Much as I delude myself that it's not in me, it seems that vein of cruelty is in my blood." A wary resignation entered his eyes as he reached the door. "I'm a member of the House of Drakos—bloodthirsty warriors who'd tamed a dragon and made its riches their own. We're a covetous, cunning lot and we like to keep our dirty secrets within our family.

"You either face the jackals for the biggest mistake we made in our lives, or you fly to Drakon with me in the lap of luxury. My limo will wait for five minutes."

CHAPTER FIVE

SNOWCAPPED MOUNTAINS AND turquoise-blue oceans—
Mia's first sight of Drakon had been as exhilarating
as it had been terrifying. Her fury with Nikandros for
railroading her into coming to Drakon with him began
to dissolve slowly as her mind churned.

A thrill-seeker and adventurer by nature and pro-
fession, he seemed to have, relatively easily, accepted
the change in direction of his life. If she hadn't had
her own hang-ups about him, if their history wasn't all
twisted with Brian in between them, would she have
fought so dirty?

Dear God, she'd pretty much told him he was good
for sex and nothing else.

Every time she'd tried to talk to him on the long
flight, he'd frozen her out.

Regret that she'd been too harsh circled her insidi-
ously.

Welcome to your new home, he'd declared in that
arrogant voice of his, his eyes shaded by the wrap-
arounds, before seeing her into a dark-tinted limo and
walking away.

He'd washed his hands of her that easily.

It was exactly the kind of relationship she'd never wanted again—full of mistrust and anger. If Nikandros thought a child would be happy growing up in such an environment, he was utterly wrong.

From the private airfield, she'd been driven to the King's Palace in the tinted limo, showed into the Grand Apartments by staff that wouldn't even meet her eyes. And left there to stew in her own anger and confusion.

That was five days ago and she hadn't heard a word from Nikandros again.

Sick of sitting on her hands waiting for Nik to show up, she'd taken to swimming in the pool in the inner courtyard, complete with a gazebo and high walls, and then walking through the gallery featuring frescoes painted as far back as the sixteenth century.

This was temporary, she kept reminding herself. Nikandros would realize what a crimp she and a baby would put in his lifestyle and let her go.

By the time the invite had arrived for lunch with the Prince, she'd lost all the guilt and the anger was back.

If this was his idea of playing happy family, she was going to give him a battle unlike anything he'd ever seen.

She pulled a round brush through her still-damp hair and left it loose around her shoulders. Dressed in black trousers and a light pink sleeveless blouse that she wore under a white jacket—she had neither better clothes nor the inclination to dress up in deference to the damned royal who had, for all intents and purposes, kidnapped her—she walked into the huge dining room.

Instantly, she felt underdressed, overwhelmed by the gold grandeur of the room.

A large oval table that could seat at least twenty stretched the length of the vast room, covered in a cream tablecloth and gleaming silver cutlery. Stained glass on high windows left the room in bright swatches of colorful light. Pink Carrara marble gleamed at her feet while gold-framed portraits hung over the walls.

Ostentatious and old-world, the room was aeons away from the adventurous, compelling man that had blown into her life like a hurricane. Nikandros no more belonged here than she, came the startling thought. In all the years, she'd never known him to be pretentious or...

No! He'd made it undeniably clear that she knew him not at all.

It took Mia a few seconds to corral her senses after the sheer magnificence of the room, and for her eyes to rest on the dark-haired figure standing near a side table gleaming with crystal decanters. Watching her silently.

She'd seen him in the pictures of late, though she would have recognized the square-jawed, high cheekboned face dripping with the kind of arrogance and power that was bred into his blood itself.

Crown Prince Andreas Drakos.

As ruthlessly conventional and devoted to Drakon, they said, as his brother was wild and reckless. And he looked like he utterly belonged in the room.

"Mrs. Morgan, thank you for accepting my invitation."

His address was to remind her who she'd been. She

instantly disliked him. He seemed like the starchy, up-tight kind of man she'd always imagined royalty to be. Puffed up with his own importance, even.

Only the dawning realization that this palace and this family would be part of her child's heritage kept her standing there. *Damn it, where the hell was Nik?*

"Little choice when you purposely misled me, Your Highness," she calmly replied.

The Crown Prince didn't blink at her retort. Without asking her, he poured her sparkling water. Which told Mia he knew.

Taking a sip, she willed her nerves to calm down at his unblinking regard. Standing next to the powerful man in the lavishly ornate room, the surreality of her situation sank like a hard rock in her stomach.

This would be her life if Nikandros had his way. She would sit here in a grandly lavish room like this one, somewhere in the palace, and wait for Nikandros to pull himself away from the thrills that filled his life, to remember that she existed.

Powerless and waiting, her heart in her hands. For Nikandros made her weak unlike any other man she'd known.

She needed to remember that he didn't like her, either. That he believed she'd driven Brian away, that she was a woman who didn't keep the vows she'd made.

That he wanted this relationship even less than she did.

The silence became stultifying as the Prince watched her. "I'm assuming the reason you invited me is not to just intimidate me with your presence, Your Highness."

Surprise glinted in the Prince's eyes.

Nikandros and his brother shared the same cut of features, and yet, there was the knowledge of having known deep joy, of happiness and anger and so many emotions lived, an uninhibited zest for life in Nik that was absent in this man's face. As if he'd never quite learned how to live.

"You have the grasp of the situation better than me, Mrs. Morgan," he added, pulling her chair for her. "Talking would be mutually beneficial."

He settled at the head of the table and signaled.

Her appetite was already growing and the food was simply delicious. Mia calmly finished everything she was served, and only then did she lift her gaze.

Her first instinct was to thank him for the lunch and walk away. To block out all this noise until she had it out with Nikandros. But that would be a coward's way out, running away and hiding. And she'd done more than enough of that in the last few years.

"Let's cut the polite chitchat. Nikandros brought me here and promptly disappeared. I would like to know to where."

"I did not expect that when I told him."

"*You?* You told him I was pregnant? How the hell would you even know?"

"A security team always keeps Nikandros under their watchful eye. Which means all of his…liaisons and their subsequent activities are also monitored for a while."

He'd called her one of many on purpose. In contrast to this hard-faced man, Nikandros appeared quite fa-

vorable. "One would think you'd be too busy with matters of state for dirty spying into your brother's affairs,
Your Highness."

"Insult and deference in the same statement. You're
something, Mrs. Morgan. Did Nik ask for a DNA test?"

Her head jerked up. The placidness of his expression
didn't slip one bit.

Mia shook her head, only now realizing how easily
Nikandros had taken her word.

"My brother has a personal fortune upward of hun-
dreds of millions, an adventure empire he's built over
the last decade and he's the scion of the illustrious
House of Drakos." Pride reverberated in his words,
against all impressions Mia had of an uncaring, almost-
indifferent picture of him. "Quite a lot hinges on your
claim, Mrs. Morgan."

"The child is his," she said with steel in her voice.
"No wonder Nikandros hated the very thought of returning here. You're full of cheap tricks, Your Highness." Their gazes held—his penetrating, hers steady.
"Why don't we make it easy? What the hell do you
want with me?"

"To ask the same question of you. What do you want
from my brother?"

"A one-way flight ticket out of his life."

"You'd leave Drakon if I arranged for it?" he
taunted, a dangerous glint in his eyes. "With no other
demand?"

Every cell in Mia jumped at the idea.

She could disappear before Nik returned. And this
time, no threat of his could make her step foot in this

blasted place again. She'd know what she was dealing with, she could resist him and his dictates for their life better.

Maybe, in time, he'd come to his senses and realize what a burden a wife and a child would be on his lifestyle.

In close confines, with her attraction to him the most irrational, unwise thing she'd ever had to face, Mia would weaken. Not her history with Brian, not her past could hold a defense against the Daredevil Prince.

Because, Nikandros Drakos was one of a kind. He'd trusted her word when another man of his ilk wouldn't have. He was determined to do the right thing by this child, at least in intention.

And so wrong for her, in every which way.

"I should accept Nik's order that we marry, just to spite you," she threw out at the Prince, while her rational mind urged her to accept his help.

Run far, far away. Before you wish for that connection again. Before you want things you can never want with him.

"Nik asked you to marry him?" He stilled with his glass raised halfway to his lips. Thick lashes couldn't quite hide his shock. "And you refused?" Some new, appraising quality entered his eyes now.

"Yes."

"Why?"

Despite the surreal situation, Mia couldn't help snorting. "Hard as it may be for you to believe, I'm not interested in a husband. Even one from your illustrious family."

The illustrious part of it was what had consumed Mia the past few days.

Ignoring the inscrutable Prince, she walked to the French doors and looked out. The air was thick with the fragrance of jasmine, and from this room high up in the palace, the royal courtyard she'd heard so much about was visible. Thousands of colored stones were formed into beautiful geometric patterns, with an open-air gallery.

Visitors were allowed inside some of the rooms once a week, she'd been told by the staff. On national holidays and other occasions, the royal family, dressed in full regalia, walked to the roof.

The King's Palace, Drakon, the man who even now was trying his best to gauge their tenuous relationship—Nikandros had turned his back on all this. Had made himself into a man in his own right.

Death-defying adventure sports or not, no one could contest his ruthless sense of business, or his meteoric rise as one of the most successful entrepreneurs who hadn't even reached thirty.

And she had reduced him to nothing better than a stud…a sperm donor. Even she, who knew very little of men and their egos, knew what an insult that had to be. Would she have liked if he'd told her she'd been a convenient screw?

A heaviness settled into her limbs.

Even with his prejudices about her marriage to Brian, Nikandros had been concerned about her the night of the press conference. A part of him had reached out to her that night, had understood what she'd lost.

And if she took this powerful man's help behind

Nikandros's back, if she ran away, it would completely destroy any hope of an amiable relationship between them. Even worse, it would be a betrayal to Nikandros. And she just couldn't do that.

The very idea of marriage made nausea rise in her throat, but for the sake of their child, Nikandros and she would have to begin somewhere. Had to put aside their differences. "I'll not leave Drakon behind his back, and definitely not with your sneaky help."

"You're not his usual sort of woman, Mrs. Morgan."

"I'm not his woman at all. That was a—" Fiery heat claiming her cheeks, Mia cut off her words. "Clearly, you know where he is. Be useful, Your Highness, and share it. I want to see him."

A brow raised on his arrogant face, just like Nikandros's did. "At a road race on the mountains of Iedas."

The most dangerous racing circuit in all of Drakon. The death toll itself on that curve was crazy.

Mia's heart thumped, a chill pervading her limbs. The grisly pictures from Brian's car accident spread before her, making her vision blurry. Torn limbs, blood everywhere, lifeless eyes... Panic rose up like an engulfing wave. She couldn't breathe, her lungs burned.

A firm hand on her shoulders guided Mia to a chair. "Head down between your knees."

Oxygen rushed into her head and she huffed, as if she'd just finished a grueling training routine. Tears pinched her eyes and nose and she held them off, just.

His chair pulled closer to hers, the Crown Prince took a seat and rubbed Mia's cold hands. God, she'd give anything to keep him safe, anything to see his blue eyes darken in the throes of passion, to see his languid mouth curve into a…

The ache closed around her throat.

"I'd kill him with my bare hands if I could right now," she mumbled, anger coming to her rescue. Anger was better than the breath-stealing fear. "I cannot do this."

Their knees almost touching, his forearms leaning on his thighs, from one breath to another, the Crown Prince transformed. A shadow of ache in his eyes, he looked nothing more than a concerned brother. "Care about Nik?" he replied with a self-deprecating twist to his hard mouth.

"I can't live through another death like my late husband's, that's all. I don't care about Nikandros."

"Worrying about Nik comes with the territory of knowing him, Mrs. Morgan. But I will tell you what I always tell myself when he goes off on one of his expeditions." Amazement and, shockingly—for Mia would've thought no other man more self-possessed or born into his role—an echo of dread filled the Crown Prince's words. "Nik has the luck of the very devil. Always.

"Did you know he'd almost been declared dead at least four times before he reached the age of sixteen?"

"What?" It was impossible to imagine that vitally masculine man as a sick child or adolescent. At death's door for any other reason except that he'd taunted it. Over and over again.

Andreas nodded, a far-off look in his eyes. "The best medical team in the world thought he wouldn't reach adolescence, much less live up to the age of thirty and go haring off to climb mountains or trek through Antarctica in the dark.

"But Nik has always defied odds and I always thought it was because of his very will, his zest for life."

Mia buried her face in her hands, forcing her nerves to calm down. Thoughts whirled and eddied, one crystallizing—the thought of this world without Nikandros in it, was unbearable.

The thought of her own life without seeing those taunting blue eyes and that wickedly curving mouth was unbearable.

And it was too late, for their fates were already tied irrevocably.

Satisfaction gleamed in Andreas's eyes. As if suddenly everything was falling into its place. "No one can deter Nikandros once he's decided on a path. If he has proposed marriage to you, he's committed to you and the baby. My brother has only ever lacked a clear path, not motivation. You have provided it."

"What the hell is going on?"

The hairs on the back of Mia's neck stood at the feral growl in that question.

With a soft pat on the back of her hands, the Crown Prince released her.

Drawing a fortifying breath, Mia turned.

Distrust glittered in Nik's eyes. Whatever silent battle raged between them, both brothers looked away finally.

Heart thumping against her chest, Mia said, "You left me here."

It was a miracle if he heard her because all the ache of knowing that he could have died any minute, or that he challenged his own mortality every day, choked her breath in her throat.

It was as if her worst nightmare had come true. Her heart had become encased in ice long ago waiting for her father to give up on his thrill. And now, she'd forever be doing the same with Nik.

Only it would be million times worse.

Because he'd already left a mark on her. All she could do was fight to stop him from taking over her heart.

"I assumed you would not have need of me so soon, Mia. At least not for a while again." Dark heat swirled in his eyes, setting the context to his words. "How may I be of service to you this time?"

Irrational fury filled every inch of her, propelling her across the room.

The endless waiting through the dark night when Brian's car had crashed, the guilt and grief, the utter waste of a life just for the thrill of it. How dare he taunt her?

He just stood there, his gaze trained on her, six feet three inches of leanly muscled, rampant male.

Mia reached him and slapped him so hard that her arm jarred at the impact.

He didn't buck or flinch or even blink. Just stood there like one of those mountains he was intent on conquering. Something dark and elemental glittered in his expression, and just as fast as it flooded her, adrenaline left her.

She swayed, feeling as if every emotion she had successfully submerged for years had returned with a vengeance. Everything was going all wrong. Her temper wasn't supposed to splinter like this; she wasn't supposed to care at all. And not for this man who played Russian roulette with his own life.

She couldn't care about Nikandros and come out intact.

Large hands incredibly gentle on her shoulders, Nikandros steadied her. The initial shock still hadn't faded from those piercing blue eyes. "Mia..."

But she had nothing to say. Locking the tears in her throat, hands clinging to his waist, Mia hid her face in his chest. Slowly, her breath lost that erratic swing.

The scent of him, woodsy and so inherently male, calmed her. He felt solid, real, utterly male.

"What did you say to frighten her?" he said into the room.

"Mrs. Morgan and I have been getting to know each other."

If anything, the hardness seemed to settle right into Nik's bones. "Leave us, Andreas."

Mia jerked back from him. "I have nothing to say to you."

"Mia."

Barely had Mia taken two steps when a woman rushed into the room. Her petite figure was neatly encased in a long-sleeved white shirt and jodhpurs. While Mia willed Nik to look at her, the woman rattled off orders to the two aides that had followed her, much like a military general barking commands. They ranged from palace administration to the Crown Prince's upcoming visit to the United States.

If not for the commanding authority in the woman's tone, Mia would have assumed it was a secretary. But no, this was the curious middle sister, Eleni Drakos. The world knew very little about the woman, even though she was a constant presence by the side of her older brother.

The moment the aides left the room, Eleni hugged Nik tight.

His harsh features softening, Nik returned the hug.

Between the two giant and gorgeously striking figures her half brothers made, the Princess looked like a plain pixie. She was short but curvaceous, with muddy brown hair that was falling out of her French braid. Everything about her felt indistinct until she smiled.

Then her face glowed, as if she was lit up from within.

Assessing, intelligent eyes turned toward Mia and greeted her with genuine warmth. "Welcome to our home, Mrs. Morgan," the Princess said, either oblivious or uncaring of the chilly atmosphere in the room.

"Thank you, Your Highness," Mia replied back automatically.

Eleni Drakos ushered everyone to sit, and waved her hand at Mia. "Please, no 'Highness' routine for me. Just Eleni. And stay. I came to meet you."

"Then, please, just Mia," Mia returned. "I hate being referred to as Mrs. Morgan, and the people who insist on calling me that."

Mia heard the chuckle from the Crown Prince like some background score, all of her awareness, her breath and her every cell hinged on the icy blue stare that was eating her up from the opposite chair.

Her palm tingled with the need to cup that bristly jaw, to see that blue ice thaw. Longing twisted deep inside of her to feel the vitality of him in the most intimate way possible.

When his gaze lifted to hers, she looked away. *What was happening to her?* For years, she'd been strong, steady, with such tight control over her emotions. And now, it was as if nothing could corral them anymore.

"I hear congratulations are in order." Grateful for Eleni's interruption, Mia tried to smile. "Nik tells me the situation is far from ideal, and I'm sure Andreas has tried to twist your mind upside down until you don't know what is right or wrong, so let me give you a little advice."

A growl emerged from Nik's throat, a sound that sent a path of fire down Mia's spine. Andreas raised his hands in mock surrender. "Nik should marry Mia if that's what he wants. After all, the House of Drakos is in sore need of heirs to pacify the public and here's a ready-made one."

Mia, Nikandros and Eleni all stared at the Crown Prince, horrified and disbelieving.

"For God's sake, stop talking about my child as if it were a commodity we ordered by mistake," Mia interjected acidly, her head swimming.

"Our child." Nik's low warning vibrated in the room. *Our child...* It was something she had to get used to.

"You don't look like you're dying soon, Your Highness," Mia added with a little acid, tugging her gaze away from Nik with Herculean strength. "And you have Eleni and Nik to follow you. How many heirs do the populace of Drakon need to be content?"

"I was born out of wedlock, and even though father adopted me, I can't inherit anything," Eleni added smoothly without missing a beat. "As for my advice, marry him, Mia. Illegitimacy becomes a boulder around one's neck if you grow up around the palace or even in Drakon. And knowing Nik, he will not let a child of his grow up without knowing him."

"My little talk with the Crown Prince made me realize I shouldn't be objecting."

He was lazily sprawled in his chair, the epitome of rebellion against every atom of tradition in the room, and yet all of Nikandros's focus stayed on her. They might as well have been alone. "First time in our lives that my brother has done something useful for me."

She made her voice cutting even as her insides twisted. "All these extreme adventure sports and races, you're going to kick the bucket soon and I'll be rid of you anyway. Why fight that fate?"

Eleni gasped but Mia forged on relentlessly, her throat like shredded glass. "Twice widowed before I'm twenty-six and all the benefits that come with being the widow of the Daredevil Prince of Drakon. At least, *our* child will have a legacy, if not a father."

"My bride-to-be is relentlessly practical, if nothing else," Nik said, his gaze drilling into Mia. He turned

to Andreas. "I'm ready to be pronounced the Hereditary Heir."

Another shock, and if she hadn't been sitting, she'd
have crumpled to the ground.

*Hereditary Heir? Did that mean he was settling
down?*

Heart pounding, Mia struggled to make sense of this.
A stupid, silly part of her even wondered if he was doing
this just to prove her wrong.

"Why are you doing this?" she burst out.

Nikandros shrugged, as if it were every day that he
considered a drastic change in his life. "It makes sense
for my life now.

"I will not tolerate any interference from you, Andreas," he continued. "We will clearly demarcate what
I'm willing to take on and what I will not touch. I know
how to make the economy boom again, and my marriage and the fact that I'm going to have a child soon
should let up the pressure the Crown Council has put
on you.

"Also convince the people of Drakon that there will
be a steady supply of heirs in the coming years."

If they'd been alone, if there wasn't a small football-
pitch-sized table separating them, Mia would have
slapped him again to wipe that arrogant smirk off his
face.

And he knew it for that gaze taunted her to try it.

"What about your company?" she threw at him.

"I'm selling it. As for dying soon," his mouth curled
into a dark smile, "no one has more respect for life and
all its myriad challenges than I.

"I've discovered a new challenge, one that comes with lifelong dividends."

"I'm not a challenge to be conquered," she retorted, her face flaming.

He shrugged, a satisfied gleam in his eyes. She'd started this in front of his siblings and it was clear he felt no shame in finishing it. "I not only intend to enjoy a long life, but a fruitful marriage so that I can teach you a lot of things. After all, a lifetime is not going to be enough for us to learn each other.

"Is it, Mia?"

Breathless and shaky, Mia could only stare as a soft heat chased the shock out of her body.

It was the last thing she'd expected of him. To share his brother's duty to Drakon. To devote himself to the life he wanted to create with her, for the sake of their child. But would he be satisfied with life as a husband and a father and his princely duties? Could a man who had chased a thrill all his life stand still for long?

Her belief that he could actually see this through, without craving that life again, fought to hold.

Was there hope? Was she actually considering this?

Was she willing to put herself in competition again with some intangible thrill he'd chase?

Because she knew as clearly as her pounding heart, that he wouldn't let her put any distance between them, even to protect herself. The chase was in his blood and he'd decided to make her his prize.

He was far more ruthless than Brian had ever been, far more calculating and dangerous even in the risks he took.

What separated Nikandros from her ex was that the Daredevil Prince played to win.

"You're no more equipped to be a father and a husband than you are to become the Prince that Drakon needs."

Her bitter words still fresh in his mind Nikandros considered and discarded the idea of chasing Mia through the corridors of the palace. Instead, he stayed put in that vast room, sifting through the reactions to his announcement.

Even in his dementia, Theos had not liked that Andreas had invited Nikandros back into the fold. That Nikandros had once walked away and succeeded in the outside world, that he'd dared to defy the great King Theos would always be held against him.

But his megalomaniac father's regime was over.

Nikandros felt the rightness of his decision in his bones. This was the answer to the restlessness that had plagued him the last year.

Eleni had been delighted; even Andreas had been smugly satisfied, which in turn unsettled Nikandros. He still didn't know if he could trust Andreas but he decided to let it be for now.

That Mia had been shocked by it was an understatement. He stroked his jaw with a smile, still feeling the imprint of her hand.

Was she still mad that he'd forced her to accompany him? That she doubted both his intentions and his capability to stay the course infuriated him, but he'd prove himself to her as he would to anyone else who'd once doubted him.

Fierce excitement filled Nik's veins. Finally, he had a chance to be the man he'd always dreamed of being when he'd been stuck in the hospice for years. When he'd looked up at the tall, commanding figures of his father and brother and wondered if he'd ever have a part in shaping Drakon.

The Hereditary Heir, he knew, could just be in titular capacity, nothing but a symbol of hope for the people, in the face of their King's dementia. But Nikandros had never been one to rest on the past laurels of his ancestors or his family.

This was his chance, his time, to leave a mark on Drakon. To achieve everything he'd ever wanted.

And he was damned if he'd let anyone—Mia or Andreas, or his mad father—stop him from becoming the Nikandros he'd been born to be.

CHAPTER SIX

NIKANDROS DIDN'T SEE Mia until midnight.

Once he'd finished with Andreas, he'd returned to his suite. But Mia hadn't been there, although one side of his cavernous closet had been filled with silk blouses and scarves and all manner of feminine things.

A subtle scent of rose had fluttered by his nostrils as he'd stood there.

Mia belonged here with him.

Dark possessive instinct he'd never known sang in his veins. However, he drew the line at smelling her clothes like a lovesick calf. Or pursuing her through the palace if she sought to hide from him.

He'd showered, shaved, dressed quickly and returned to work. Now that he and Andreas were on the same page, he couldn't wait to begin. The challenge of conquering Drakon, the thrill of putting all his plans into motion, after all these years—the rightness of this was more thrilling than scaling the highest mountain peak or trekking through a dangerous jungle.

The logistics of moving his business to Drakon—the bare bones of it for he had already sold chunks of it—took up most of his afternoon.

By nightfall, Nik was gritting his teeth at the amount of bureaucratic red tape he'd had to get through to find out rights over acres of mountain land that should have belonged to the royal family.

He was meeting with a land surveyor and an architect tomorrow to see two different parcels of land where he intended to build a five-star ski resort and a luxury adventure club. They'd have to ease up on their banking and taxing laws for money to pour into Drakon.

It was well past two in the morning when he'd returned to his suite. He found Mia sleeping on the chaise longue in the sitting lounge.

Had she fallen asleep waiting for him?

The paperback next to her and the steel water bottle she always carried around said she'd intended to sleep there.

If she thought they were sleeping separately...

Feet rooted to the spot, he stared at her.

The thin shawl she'd draped over her body twisted around her, baring long, sleek, honey-gold legs. Legs she had wrapped around his waist to hold on to him when he'd pounded into her heat.

Instant need pooled in his lower belly as his gaze moved up from the V between her thighs where he could see pink panties—*Christos*, had any woman tormented him like this ever?—up that taut midriff to breasts that had seemed like they'd been made to fit in his hands.

Something else twisted in his chest as his gaze reached her face.

Wavy brown hair settled into a cloud around her face, and wearing a worn-out old tee that said Miami Heat, the name of her old soccer team, she looked incredibly young and irresistibly innocent.

Young and innocent, not words he'd associated with Mia.

With her career success and her much-speculated-over marriage to Brian and the poised quality she'd always possessed, Nikandros had forgotten how young she was.

The women he knew of her age—friends and girl-friends alike—were still experimenting with their career paths. They partied hard, sampling everything life had to offer, flitted just as easily from lover to lover as Nikandros had done. But Mia, for as long as he'd known her, had been incredibly devoted to soccer, had always lived life from behind a wall of cool aloofness as if nothing could touch her.

It was only on the soccer field that the real woman came through—or when she was trading insults with him, he realized. Brian had told him again and again how Mia had frozen him out, but she seemed to have no problem provoking Nik or losing her own temper with him.

And that she was different with him—the blaze that came into her eyes, the faint fury that made her mouth tremble when he challenged her—it entertained him no end.

There was a freshly scrubbed beauty to her features in repose. Long lashes cast crescent shadows on those high cheekbones. The smudges under her eyes told Nik something he wouldn't have ever believed.

Christos, had she been crying?

Nikandros will leave me twice widowed before I'm twenty-six.

Her eyelids fluttered continuously, like the wings of a butterfly, her sleep as restless as the blood in his veins.

As Nik watched, she shifted on the chaise, pushed the shawl away with an agitated quiver. A soft groan fell from her mouth, a line flitting between those arched eyebrows. Her hand moved to her back and rubbed.

He'd seen enough.

Mind made up, Nikandros lifted her. Instantly, her arms wound around his neck, and her breasts pushed against his chest. In a cloud of warmth and softness, he swallowed at the bolt of lust that arrowed down his spine.

Gritting his teeth, he carried her to his bedroom and gently lowered her onto the bed.

The moment her pliant body hit the bed, her eyes drifted open. Determined to keep her in the bed if he had to bind her to it, he sat down. Her tart mouth stretched into an inviting bow just as her sleep-kissed eyes widened.

A shadow of fear and something else. And a soft mew of sound, edged with pain, fell from her mouth.

She'd flay him for sure, and yet he'd never known such heated anticipation as he waited, such a thrill coursing through his veins that he'd never known the like in all his adventures.

Her nostrils twitched delicately, and she moved up on the bed in a sensuous, silky slither that would have been a sultry invitation from any other woman. "You're back," she whispered then. Her smile was still sleep-mussed, her expression not completely awake.

She was dreaming, Nik realized.

Shaking fingers trailed over his face—his temple first, and then his nose, stopped short of his mouth. Lust punched into him, his head swimming in the soft heat of her. She cupped his jawline and traced it with her thumb in slow, soft strokes that reached his mouth every time, and then stopped.

Locking his muscles tight against the overwhelming urge to bury his mouth in the inviting crook of her neck, Nik closed his eyes. As if answering his body's scream, her fingers moved to his mouth. On and on, back and forth, she pressed and prodded and traced his lips until he felt burned through and through.

When she tugged at his forearms, he went, a slave to the call of her body. Tucking herself into him, her bottom nestling against his groin was pure torture. She folded his arm over her and gripped him tightly. "Don't die on me, Nikandros. God, please don't." Another shiver, another keen cry as if it were ripping her apart. "I won't be able to bear it."

Utter stillness came over him. The pain in her words was far too real to ignore. "Mia?" he said, pushing away a lock of hair from her forehead. "*Agapita*, you're having a nightmare."

"There was an accident again," she whispered, her words thick and unclear. "You were lying under that wreckage.

"Your body—" she breathed in a huge gulp "—bent

at strange angles. And you won't smile. However many times I call you, you won't answer."

She shook so violently that Nik held her down with his arm. "Shh...*pethi mou*, I'm here, I'm fine, Mia," he whispered against her temple.

"You are?" As if to answer her own question, she brought his hand to her mouth and kissed the center of his palm. The wetness from her eyes stung Nikandros, sharper than her accusations during lunch.

Was that why she'd slapped him? Had she been worried he would die like Brian? She'd gone through it all alone then. Nik had mourned too and resented her for getting what she wanted—an out from the marriage.

Christos, he didn't realize how much resentment he'd harbored against her.

His mind whirled in every direction. He'd so easily decided that her marriage to Brian had left no scars. That she'd driven him away, that the failure of their marriage had been solely her fault.

All he knew of their marriage was from Brian. And the news of his affairs.

While every inch of his own body solidified into rock to ward off the desire coming at him in waves, her own body softened. Her breath fell into a deep rhythm.

Nik had no idea how long he waited like that, on the edge of the bed, cocooning her body with his, breathing in the scent of hers.

Only now did he see what lingered under his dirty accusations. He didn't want Brian's shadow between them. He didn't want to know what had happened between them, or who had been culpable. He couldn't hold the things Brian had told him about her or their marriage.

Every time she mentioned his name, it felt as if the past was on a repeat. As if Nik's role in her life was murkier. As if he were fighting a ghost from the past.

Which meant he didn't have the right to pull that punch on her.

When he left the bed in the early hours of dawn, all he had was more doubts about Mia and a raging need for another cold shower.

Nikandros had no time the next couple of days to ponder his exchange with a half-asleep Mia. All hell seemed to have broken loose around the news that the Daredevil of Drakon had returned. And had brought along a woman.

The same woman who stormed into the bathroom while Nikandros was in the shower. Dressed in a simple shift dress in lemon yellow, she looked like the wild sunflowers that grew at the foothills of the mountain range in Drakon.

Through the stained glass, he could see the tense line of her shoulders, the stillness that had come over her the moment she'd realized where she'd marched into.

Despite the impasse they seemed to be at, Nik grinned. He took a step back and flashed his side at her. "You're welcome to join me, Mia."

Her eyes darkened and roved over him, her breath shallow. "This is only an attempt to talk to you. You're gone before I wake up, you return after I fall asleep."

He felt like a strutting peacock, not that he minded. "If you want the full frontal, all you have to do is ask."

Opening the door wider, he turned until she could see his front and his raging erection, which only lengthened when her hungry gaze fell on it.

Like a spinning top, she turned around, presenting him with her back. But not quick enough to hide the raw want that had flashed across her face. "I'm interested in a talk. Not a reenactment of *Magic Mike*."

"What is *Magic Mike*?"

"A movie about male strippers. Another career path I'm sure you'd succeed at."

"That sounds like a compliment," he shouted at her.

Dialing the water to a cold blast, he cursed her, his body and anything else he could think of. Stepping out of the shower, he walked close by her, and then grabbed a large towel.

Without bothering to cover himself.

"Put on your clothes, Nikandros."

"You're the one who barged into the bathroom. And really, Mia, it's nothing you haven't seen or touched or stroked or kissed. No, I'm wrong. You didn't kiss my—"

Her hand slapped over his mouth with such force that he fell back against the wall and she toppled against him. Her hands fell on his cold flesh, her breath heating it up within seconds. The rasp of her nipples against his chest made his erection draw up tight between the heated press of their bodies.

He pushed her hand away and crushed her mouth with his. God, he needed her taste more than anything he'd needed in life.

When she gasped, he took advantage and plunged his tongue inside. Licked the tempting cavern of her mouth. Her moan egged him on, her nails raking over his chest painfully.

Lust rode him hard, sending bolts of pleasure down his thighs.

Fisting his hands in her hair, he angled her mouth the way he wanted it. No, needed it. Mia poured herself into the voluptuous kiss, digging her teeth into his lower lip and licking into his mouth in an erotic game he would never tire of.

No submission. No retreat. No rationality.

Just simple, fiery need.

Christos, she'd learned what he liked. And she was giving it to him with a ferocity that made his balls tight. That made him growl at the back of his throat.

This time, he was going to take her hard and furious, teach her that she couldn't dismiss him that easily. Not from her body at least.

Her leg wound around his thigh, the apex between her legs pressed against his bare thigh. Sinuous heat pooled low in his groin at the warmth radiating from her sex. He rubbed his flesh against her core all the while licking and stroking every inch of her mouth with his.

Her groan rasped against his senses, the instinctive tilt and thrust of her hips going straight to his arousal.

You're an incredibly generous lover. Not marriage material.

And yet he could take her again, standing like this, against the wall in the steam-filled bathroom. He could plunge into her wet heat again and again and she would not resist him.

With willpower he didn't even know he possessed,

he pushed her away from him. Gently and yet firmly. It was more painful than a limb being ripped out of its socket. Which had happened to him once.

His breath was bellowing in his ears, his erection painfully hard.

Mouth swollen and parted, eyes glossed over, she stumbled and reached out behind her. Hair mussed up around her face, she was all woman. "Nik?"

He rubbed his thumb against that lush lower lip, the moisture beaded there reminding him of other places on her he wanted to touch and lick. "Would you like me to continue, Mia?"

Deep color suffused her cheeks and her gaze lifted to his. She blinked, and then gasped, and pushed away from him. "I…that…"

"I could take you against that wall, *agapita*, but I have no more interest in playing your stud."

She fled.

Inside his closet, he pulled on black trousers, his body aching with a hum that wouldn't quit. That didn't feel like a win.

It felt like a cheap trick.

And his disgusting behavior a decade ago notwithstanding, cheap tricks were not his thing.

Yet, somehow, Mia, with an annoying regularity seemed to sink under Nik's skin, bringing out all kinds of urges he shouldn't be giving in to.

She was waiting for him in the bedroom, leaning against the huge bed.

"I want to move to a different suite."

He was in no mood for an argument, but he'd also seen the flash of fear in her eyes before she'd masked it with that aloofness.

Was she still thinking he would die like Brian?

"My fiancée will sleep in my suite." He slid a glance over her. There was a wet patch on her chest. The sight of tight nipples pushing against the wet fabric made Nik's mouth water.

He walked back into his closet and picked out a neatly folded T-shirt from her side of the closet. He threw it at her carelessly. "You need to change."

"My dress is perfectly f—" She looked down and clutched the tee to her chest like a lifeline.

Her nipples distended, pushed against the wet fabric. Mia groaned and closed her eyes, willing her body to cool down. But the throbbing he had awoken between her legs wouldn't ease.

And since undressing in front of him or away from him would become another small battle, she threw the shirt at his broad, gleaming back. Found meager satisfaction because of course, he was right.

It galled her how many things he'd been right about.

She owed him an apology. But all her good intentions fled the minute she neared him. He aroused her, and riled her and yet seemed to be utterly in control.

Mortification painting her cheeks, Mia breathed easy when he buttoned his shirt and tucked it into his trousers. There wasn't an ounce of extra flesh in his body. Sleek and defined, he reminded her of a finely sculpted statue. With just as fine an ass.

"This is not easy for me, Nikandros."

"You think it is for me?" Whirling around, he came to stand by her, his chin lifted.

Freshly showered, he smelled of skin and soap and sex.

After a couple of clueless minutes, Mia edged forward to stand in the cradle of his legs. It was impossible to knot his tie without leaning into him, without feeling the rock-hard strength of his thighs against her own.

"Tell me why it's not."

His Adam's apple bobbed up and down when her fingers grazed his throat. "What is not what?"

"Why this—" she moved her hands between her chest and his, and again had the impression that he was tense "—is hard for you when you're getting your way in everything. When the whole world seems to be arranging itself to your satisfaction.

"Instead of putting it across in more sensible terms, I played into your hands with that cheap remark. Which gave you just enough ammunition to threaten me so ruthlessly."

"And which cheap remark are you referring to?"

While it was tempting to gloss over it, Mia didn't want a repeat of her marriage to Brian. At least Nikandros dealt in honesty—even of the searing kind, and she owed him the same. "The cheap remark about you being good enough only for sex.

"It's not as if I'm a regular femme fatale to pick out men for sex and coolly wave goodbye.

"What I meant to say, was that we seemed to bring the worst out in each other."

When he stayed curiously silent, she continued. "In all

the years we've been on the peripheries of each other's lives, I never attributed that ruthlessness to you. Charm and your masculinity seemed to be enough for you to get your way."

"I don't know whether I'm being insulted or complimented."

"You were a different man when you threatened me with media exposure if I didn't quietly come to Drakon."

He sighed, some of the tension releasing from him. "All my life, I have fought for a place in the scheme of things. Here, in Drakon. With my father. With my brother. With Eleni.

"And when I didn't find one, I went and made one for myself.

"I do not take well to being denied what I want, Mia. To being used in the name of one thing or the other. It brings out the worst in me. And I can't apologize for something I would do again."

"But isn't that what we both did, Nik? Used each other that night?"

"Yes. But there was honesty between us, yes? No hidden agendas. No manipulations. And however that night started, the pregnancy throws it all out, does it not?"

She nodded, for the first time seeing what he meant. When push came to shove, he'd adjusted to the situation better and first. The daredevil had shown more predictability than her—it was a galling point.

"Is that why it's not easy being here?" she prompted, realizing how easily she'd stereotyped him into just one role.

"The palace, the staff, every protocol is a reminder that I never fit my father's idea for his son, to wonder if Andreas means his word that he wants me here, a reminder of things I'd rather forget." He rubbed a hand over his face. "I walked out once because of the distrust, the manipulations, the lack of confidence in everything I stood for.

"I will not fight the same fight with you too, Mia."

"No, nor will I." She finished with his tie, and placed her hands over his chest. His heart thumped under her palm. "You…can't imagine what I felt knowing you were off racing that death trap again. I won't be of any use to our child wondering when I'm going to get the news that…" She bent her head to his chest, unable to finish the ghastly thought again.

She didn't want to say anything that would disturb this tentative truce. It was the first time they weren't tearing off each other's clothes or tearing chunks out of each other.

"That race had been scheduled months ago," he said, his tone gentling. "My company and the shareholders and my fans expect me to show up to work."

"That's work?"

"For me, yes." He leaned against the bed, beside her. A lock of unruly hair fell forward, diluting the easy confidence he wore like a second skin. "But my participation will be purely from behind my desk from now on and from a shareholder's point of view."

It was as if a boulder that had been sitting on her chest had been lifted away. Like the wings of a caged bird were free to flap again. "You're serious?"

"Yes."

She so desperately wanted to believe, to let that hope that was fluttering in her chest loose. The yearning to imagine a future with him and their baby filled with happiness, it was so acute that it hurt to breathe. She didn't even want a lot—she just wanted loyalty and a little bit of affection.

But God, she'd been down this path before. She'd heard a thousand promises and believed them every single time. Only to have her heart crushed. Only to fall and splinter into fragments. In the end, she'd lost her ability to trust even herself.

She'd so thoroughly locked away her own instincts that she hadn't seen beneath Brian's surface charm or that ambition and greed could drive him into a hole.

"But, of course, you do not believe me." The wariness in his tone dissipated the camaraderie of just a few moments.

"Andreas told me about your childhood illness. About how it spurred you into challenging yourself. I just find it hard to trust that you'll shrug that crazy drive of yours now because you've a sudden—"

His jaw clenched so tight that Mia's words drifted away. "It was resentment that my father thought me the runt of his litter that I sought to banish from my life. While I succeeded beyond my wildest dreams, now I'm restless. Uncomfortable in this skin I've grown.

"What remains when every challenge is conquered? When you realize all you've done is run away from your own shadow?"

"Emptiness." The answer burst forth from her lips.

It was all she'd known in the months after her injury. Her marriage had self-destructed, her career in ruins; only then had Mia realized she had nothing of meaning in her life. No family, no lasting friendships—one way or another, she'd alienated herself from every good thing in life.

She grabbed Nik's hand on an impulse and held it tight. "I understand, Nikandros. More than you think." She pressed her face into his hand, hope twisting through her painfully. "I so want to believe you." It was the first glimpse she'd showed him of what was in her heart.

He lifted her hand to his mouth, pressed a tender kiss to the back of it. When he looked at her, the moment glittered with exuberant promise, a fervent connection with another soul like she'd never known.

"Working to turn the machine of Drakon's economy is not an easy task, Mia. I have Andreas's cooperation but only just. I'm going to need every skill I have in hand," he said, tapping on the back of her hand. Breaking the intimate spell weaving around them. "You'll stay in my apartments, sleep in my bed. Enough time to get used to the idea of marriage."

For once, it wasn't the idea of marriage that tripped her up. "You said your obsession with me...wanting me was over. Even now, it was you that pulled away." A rush of heat filled her cheeks but Mia held his gaze. "I would enjoy shocking you, Nikandros, if I knew the reason for it."

He smiled then, and it was such a beautiful sight that her heart ached. She hoped their child inherited that devilish smile. And his unquenchable zest for life. And his unending courage. And his capacity for loyalty.

She was slowly beginning to see the puzzle of his childhood, understood that Andreas and his father had isolated Nikandros, if not worse. And yet he was here when his brother needed him.

"I'm shocked because you admitted that you want me in so many words. There is such a lack of artifice in you when you speak."

"A lack of sophistication, you mean?" she said, forcing a smile. That she was nothing like Nikandros's usual girlfriends was a pill she was slowly beginning to swallow. Not stylish enough. Not educated enough. Not fun enough, if his antics last year with an underwear model could be counted. "It isn't as if the proof isn't there right in front of us."

"I'm a healthy male in his prime and I have needs."

"You sound like a commercial for Viagra."

Again that laugh came. Grooves in his cheeks, stubborn nose flaring, eyes shining, he made her heart thunder in her chest. "I think we have proved conclusively that I do not need Viagra, *pethi mou*.

"And I have a moderately attractive woman—" she gasped and thumped his shoulder, and the devil grinned "—who shall be my wife soon. Those needs *arise* in close quarters with you." He waggled his eyebrows as if his meaning wasn't clear enough and Mia burst out laughing.

The man could charm the color blue out of the sky.

"So," he continued, his gaze hitched on her mouth, "it makes sense to satisfy those needs with her, rather than trawl through pubs and clubs, playing the singles scene again.

"Celibacy and I do not get along."

And just like that, with that masculine, egotistical statement, he broke the tenuous connection. Mia raised stricken eyes to him. "You'd put me through that kind of relationship again? Make me wonder, as I did with Brian, if you're in some other woman's arms, kissing…"

There was only so much time and distance he was willing to give her. After all these years, being near Mia, having her in the same bed—*Christos*, even the pillows and sheets smelled like her now—and telling his body that he couldn't really have her, was messing up his head.

"If you insist on different suites and stupid rules, yes," he said stubbornly.

She shrank back as if he'd struck her. Turned around and fled.

Nik breathed out another curse—damn it, where was his sense—and followed her.

Andreas had always said he'd been born chock-full of charm, and it had been true. Nikandros had always so easily charmed things out of women—sweets from the kitchen maids, midnight strolls through the secret passageways in the palace from his besotted nanny, clothes and that sense of uppitiness from many a woman… But when it came to Mia, the one woman with whom he wanted a meaningful relationship, a sane life, he had as much charm as a toad.

"Mia, wait…"

"I won't make the same mistake I made with Brian.

If you insist on tying us into a marriage, fine. But I will not take your cheating lying down. Thanks to you, I have discovered I've just as much libido as any other woman, or man for that matter. I will wait for as long as this baby comes."

Every muscle in his body tensed up. "And then what?"

Her gaze met his, full of defiance. "And then... I... I'm going to get my body back, I'm going to get back to my career, and if a man should show interest in me, I'm going to take him on.

"I'm not going to live a celibate life, hoping you'll not stray, hoping you'll see the error of your ways."

His head was pounding now. "You're threatening me with adultery before you even agree to marry me?"

"Which is exactly what you just did. I told you, I'm through playing the victim."

Rubbing at his temples, Nik sighed. He'd lost any ground he'd gained with that reckless statement. He didn't even want another woman—he wanted Mia. So what was that if it wasn't his stupid ego talking?

But the idea of Mia with any other man, it stilled everything within him.

"What I said was utterly stupid. I've never cheated on a girlfriend even."

"Brian would never ever apologize, even when he knew he was in the wrong."

His temper flared. Gritting his teeth, he corralled that first wave of reaction. "The worst thing you could do to kill any chance we have of making this work is measure me against him.

"Or any other man.

"I've spent my entire life being compared to…" A curse flew from him. "I'm not Brian and I don't care to know how I come up against him.

"This is you and me and the baby, Mia. No one else."

As if she could sense the anger in him, she took his hands in hers. "If you want me to give this a real try, then you have to, too."

"I brought you here and announced to my family that I intend to marry you. That's more than you've given me."

"Yes. But you want it for this baby, Nikandros. That's not good enough. Our relationship will be nothing but a burden on a child if we can't stand each other."

He was living proof of how a parent could mess up the child. "What do you want from me?"

"I want time. I don't want to talk of marriage until I know we can live with each other, without shredding each other."

She didn't ask for love. She didn't ask for undying devotion. What she did ask, he could damn well give to her. It wasn't as if he had enormous practice with relationships. *Thee Mou*, he couldn't even look at his own family without resentment flaring and the longest relationship he'd had with a woman was three months because he'd been in Antarctica for two of those months.

He just didn't do well with expectations, so he'd always been alone. And it had worked well with his lifestyle, because for all his appeal, no woman wanted a man who constantly looked for the next thrill. Who was determined to run far and fast from the one place he'd always desperately wanted to belong to. From himself even.

But with Mia, every tenet he lived by went out the door. He wanted to tie her to him so fast and so tight that nothing could disrupt it.

"I want to know this will work before we—"

"That's impossible," he interrupted her, noting the thread of anxiety in her tone. "That's like wanting to know the outcome of a game before you even play it."

"I hate risks. In games and in life. And you…you take risks no man would ever even consider."

"Fine. You have time. But I will use every weapon in my arsenal to persuade you. And I believe you could not call me cocky if I say I have the best weapon of all."

CHAPTER SEVEN

MIA SPENT THE next few weeks trying to carve a routine for herself and to cling only to the outer fringes of the royal family. But the royal siblings, as they were called by the media, sucked her in like a whirlpool.

She could have fought Nikandros, had become adept at handling even the Crown Prince's sneaky little manipulations to convince her that Nikandros was a catch, but it was Eleni Drakos that seemed to be made of immovable will.

She'd signed Mia up for etiquette lessons. And for a new wardrobe. And history lessons about Drakon and the damned dragon that a band of fierce warriors had apparently taken down a millennium ago.

Despite her numerous shortcomings to becoming a princess according to Eleni, Mia enjoyed the dinners. Even the constant tension between calm, self-controlled Andreas, who rarely betrayed his thoughts and the hot-headed, impulsive Nikandros, who was already chafing at the constraints of "damned bureaucracy" as he called it.

Of course, when Mia had asked Eleni what had transpired between the brothers to make them so wary of each other, she'd clammed up.

But every time she sat down to dinner with them, Mia felt the estrangement with her own sister, Emmanuela, like a physical ache. Her older sister couldn't understand Mia's decision for walking away all those years ago, hadn't understood that for Mia, soccer had been a way to fight the constant disappointments and the soul-crushing hope that came after each of her father's promises.

Family was everything to them and Mia had simply walked away from it when it had become too hard. A pattern she was beginning to see in every aspect of her life, she thought with a sinking realization. When Brian had died in that accident and Emmanuela had called her, Mia had found it incredibly hard to break past the grief and self-pity she'd suffered. In the end, they'd talked for barely a couple of minutes and like strangers, instead of sisters who'd once adored each other.

Mia had hung up before the topic of their mom had even come up.

But seeing Nik and Andreas struggle to create something new while there was clearly a huge source of tension between them gave her fresh hope.

She was going to have a baby. Wouldn't Emmanuela welcome the news? Wouldn't her mom be excited that Mia was finally in a good place, that she was going to be an *abuela*?

The urge to pick up the phone and call them was an ache inside her. Just as soon as she figured out what she was going to say. As soon as she armed herself with enough courage. For the possibility that Mia had left it too long, had done the unforgivable and it wasn't possible to mend what had been fractured.

In the meantime, she spent her days steeped in the history and grandeur of the King's Palace.

With its stunning galleries and frescoes, it was an art education in itself. There were pleasure gardens; Drakonian soil was fertile with a vast array of exotic flowers and trees.

A library that could easily swallow a soccer field, books as far as the eye could see. Mia had gotten lost in there the first time Nikandros had brought her, marveling at leather-bound first editions, ranging from European history to world politics and the average romance paperback. When she had happily plucked a few from the shelves—they had always been her companions against loneliness—Nikandros had laughed and said his *maman* would approve of Mia.

Apparently, the romance selection had been added at the behest of the French-born Camille.

Combined, the palace, the gardens and the library were a treasure trove that kept Mia busy. Her career-ending injury and Brian's death had come stacked together at her and she'd spent the whole year feeling sorry for herself.

Only now, under the Mediterranean sun, was she beginning to realize how many things that she loved doing had been pushed aside because she'd been training and playing soccer since she'd been sixteen. She didn't even have a college degree, something she could now at least consider.

But the joy in each morning, the anticipation that bubbled over in her tummy when she looked forward to a quiet evening in their suite, the pleasure that drenched her when she saw a red rose on their bed sometimes—it was all due to the dance she was engaging in with the devil. Their relationship, while she knew he'd never agree to call it friendship, was changing, growing.

Sometime in the second week, Mia learned that the word *subtlety* was not in the man's dictionary when she'd requested of Nikandros a patch of the space somewhere near the herbal gardens the kitchen maintained. She had always loved mucking about in the gardens with her mother, coaxing fragile flowers and plants, and she wanted to get back to it. It felt like a connection she could reestablish before she could actually gather the courage to call her mom.

What she'd been presented with the next morning had been about a quarter of an acre, and a barn full of farm implements and a hundred varieties of garden soils and an army of servants all lined up neatly next to said barn.

"Is it not what you envisioned?" Nik had asked her at her continued silence.

"Do you want to turn me to farming?" she'd asked, tongue-in-cheek.

He had frowned, then stared at her, a grumpy expression clouding his face. "You asked for land. Andreas and I discussed it and decided this piece of land would work perfectly for you. It is prohibited from the general public."

"Uh-huh, uh-huh… *A patch of land* is what I believe I said, Nik. Not this…acreage." She burst out laughing.

He glared at her. "You could have asked for diamonds or jewelry or for shares in the newest couture house in Drakon, but no… You had to ask for land and manure and soil. How in blazes would I know how much is too much?"

"Unless you want me to provide produce for palace consumption, this is too much."

Hands slipped into his pockets, he'd held her gaze with his, and then looked away.

"No one has ever asked me for a gift, Mia. I wanted to give you what you asked for. I want you and our child to have everything under the sun. I want this to work."

If there had been a moment Mia thought her heart would burst out of her chest, that had been it. Her heart had fluttered like a butterfly.

The afternoon sun kissing the strong angles of his face, his white shirt undone to reveal a tanned throat, wavy hair falling over one brow, Nikandros had never looked more like a fantastic dream come true.

What did he see in her, she kept asking herself, except that she wasn't falling to her knees at the prospect of being his wife and that she carried his child. How could she even hope to continue to hold his attention, to compete against the reckless, hair-raising lifestyle he'd lived all these years?

Dragging him with her while the staff watched with a range of expressions, she had picked up plant markers and showed him.

He'd frowned at the rectangle. "That's it?"

His confusion goaded some imp within. "Bigger, Nikandros, is not always better."

Piercing blue eyes full of the very devil, he had caged her against the barn door, and whispered, "I think you need to be reminded you have it the other way, *pethi mou*. Bigger can lead to better," before he bit her lower lip in front of the whole damn staff.

It was something she'd never get used to—staff waiting on her hand and foot, intruding on every hour of her life, she decided. Until the blue-eyed devil stroked her upper lip with a wicked brush of his tongue.

Mia immediately gasped and he nuzzled into her mouth with a deep groan that sent shivers down her spine. Strong hands clasped her cheeks for his deeper pressure. The very land beneath her feet seemed to move as a flood of pleasure filled Mia.

There was no hard destination with this kiss, no urgent heat building them up.

It was a lazy layering of sensation upon sensation over her senses, filling her up with the potent masculinity of the man that made her femininity sing.

Afternoon sun warmed their bodies, the fragrance of herbs teasing her nostrils, and Nikandros's long, lazy kiss, her veins infused with molten honey.

By the time he'd let her up for air, Mia groaned in protest, leaning against his hard body for support. His wicked mouth buried in the crook of her neck. "There's cushiony hay in the barn, Mia. I took the full tour before deciding if this was right for you." Her pulse jumped at the lazy flick of his tongue. "And I will make sure it doesn't scratch you."

She felt his slow smile against her skin and almost caved. When Mia had pointed out that they'd both agreed to not muddy their tenuous truce with sex, he'd cursed soundly and bit out that he should be given a bloody award for his patience.

Not that he didn't twist the rules they'd set in place.

The rogue touched her, fondled her, literally rubbed against her every chance he got. Told her just as often, in wicked, wanton words, what he was going to do to her and with her, and inside her, as soon as she caved.

It was infuriatingly frustrating, for Mia was beginning to agree with him that it was a stupid idea. But sex would only muddle things between them. Sharing that raw intimacy with Nikandros again, where he left nothing for Mia to hide behind, she wasn't ready for it at all.

Long fingers sank into her hair and tugged her chin up. The laughter was gone from his eyes, replaced by something else. His mouth became that hard curve that she didn't like. "I'll be gone for two weeks," he said into the stretched silence finally.

Faint alarm tripped through her. "Where are you going?"

"I have to meet investors. I'm going to turn Drakon into the world's luxury destination." A fire blazed in his blue eyes. "I'm going to make everyone's head turn." He faintly shook with the challenge of it all.

"You already turn heads, Nikandros," she admitted grudgingly. "Too many, if you ask me."

Just the number of "family friends" who had come to visit him, with their daughters in tow, was enough to make Mia's gut knot.

Women would always swarm to him, she'd realized one evening, when she'd walked into his office and found him surrounded by two young women, who Eleni had told her with obvious relish were the daughters of a cabinet minister and of a powerful Drakonite family.

Mia had quietly backed away from the door, but not before Nikandros had seen her leave. She wanted their relationship kept secret for a while, but it had taken every ounce of willpower she'd had to not barge in there and pronounce that the daredevil was taken.

By her.

She saw the memory of it darken his eyes now. "You're the one who wants to hide this."

Wrapping her fingers around his wrists, she held her ground, even as the intensity of his gaze probed her as if he wanted to see into the heart of her. His hesitation when he was used to saying whatever came to him, made her frown.

His thumb traced the line of her jaw. It wasn't a soft stroke, a lover's touch. It felt like he wanted to leave his brand on her. "I do not like leaving you here."

The significance of that softly uttered statement fell like a minefield in the pleasant silence. Was it her he didn't trust? Or someone else?

"I gave you my word, Nikandros," she said, finally understanding the shadows in his eyes. Had she thought him a relatively simple man? The joke was on her.

He nodded but still didn't let go. "Andreas will—"

"The Crown Prince is the least of my worries, Nikandros. If I can take on Eleni and stay standing, believe me, Andreas is nothing."

Laughter burst out of him, traveling through her like a pure bolt of energy. "You're not scared of her, are you?"

"She has signed me up for etiquette lessons, history of Drakon and for fittings for a new wardrobe. If I didn't know she means well, I'd hate her.

"Apparently, I don't possess a single quality a future princess should."

"You know what you should do if you want her to like you."

She sighed. The appearance of those women in Nik's office had made Mia dwell on more than one thing. "I'm nothing like the women your family would have expected you to marry. I don't possess the sophistication or the connections to recommend myself, Nikandros.

"If you resent my lack of—"

"My family, if not the world, never even expected me to marry, Mia. You know I don't give a damn about the traditions that shackle me. And if you want to get Eleni off your back, I have a secret."

"What?" she asked eagerly, desperate for anything.

"Make me happy."

"And what can I do that will make the Daredevil Prince of Drakon happy?" she taunted him, every inch of her fizzing with delight.

He brushed another furious kiss on her mouth and walked away without answering her question.

But she knew what he wanted and she was beginning to hate herself for not falling into this relationship headlong. For not being impulsive enough or daring enough for the Daredevil Prince.

Touching her fingers to her trembling lips, Mia stared at his retreating form.

With each passing day, she felt more and more like that teenage Mia who had adored him from afar.

He was committed to her, showed every indication of wanting their relationship to work. It was as if a crazy daydream had suddenly burst into furious life and Mia was terrified of taking part in it.

When Mia returned to their suite after her morning run—it had been thirteen days since Nikandros had left and she'd barely exchanged two words with him on the phone—it was as if she'd stepped into a hot zone. Papers were strewn about on every surface of the sitting lounge as if someone had thrown them around in a fit of anger.

Two aides stood mute outside the bedroom door, pretending to death as if they couldn't hear the two voices—one raising hell and the other implacably, immovably soft—arguing inside.

Wiping the sweat pouring down her neck, she signaled for them to leave. Where was Eleni when her interference was desperately needed? Mia hated confrontations, but there was nothing to do but barge into that room. It almost felt like she'd been waiting for this to occur since she'd arrived.

She'd taken barely two steps when Andreas walked out into the lounge, stared at her and quietly walked out.

Mia walked into the bedroom and found Nikandros standing at the French doors looking out into the courtyard behind. Dressed in a white shirt and black trousers, he was a study in masculine perfection. The tension that seemed to radiate from him stilled Mia.

He turned as if sensing her presence.

The inherent masculinity of him took her breath away.

His tie was loosened and the first few buttons on his shirt undone. Sleeves pushed back revealed dark hair on skin she knew would somehow be taut and yet satiny.

Soft tingles started in so many points in her body, making her aware of his thorough perusal of her. Heat spreading up her neck, she lifted her eyes.

Mia caught the shadow of some dark emotions before he chased it away with one of his trademark smiles. "You have been well?" he asked politely.

The distance between them suddenly felt like it could span the ocean. Mia wanted to go to him desperately, wanted to pull his head down and touch her mouth to his, dissipate the dark cloud of emotion surrounding him, but there was such a forbidding air about him that she held the impulse back.

"I'm doing fine," she replied. The man who'd kissed her so lazily, the man who'd teased and taunted her for weeks was nowhere in sight.

"When did you return?"

"Around four in the morning." Deep grooves settled on either side of his mouth.

"Why didn't you come to bed?"

A gleam of desire made his eyes glitter, rendering them sharp in the dark planes of his face. Only then did she realize how *possessive* she sounded.

Another shrug. "I was very…eager to discuss some things with the Crown Prince."

Every time he said *Crown Prince* in that derisive tone, Mia knew something was wrong between them. "You have been talking all these hours?"

"We talked for a while. Andreas freaked out. I yelled and walked out. Just as I was about to leave—" his mouth became a hard line "—I remembered that I have a *woman in here pregnant with my child*." The exaggerated title stung Mia like a scrape of skin. "By the time I came back, you'd left for your run. Then Andreas found me here again. Anything else you want me to account for?"

"No," she threw back, lifting her chin. But for all her outward stand, anxiety twisted in her gut.

It was only now, when he was so completely shuttered away from her that she realized how much she missed his raw honesty. He was like an opaque glass standing in front of her, redirecting everything back at her.

An empty echo. She'd been in that same place too many times, found it impossible to break through to Brian and before that, her dad. And she was damned if she let Nikandros put distance between them now.

The blue of his eyes flared when she came to a stop, their bodies not quite touching. "Your trip, did it not go well?"

He wrapped his hand around his nape and leaned back against the wall. With the sleeves pushed back, the dial of his watch caught flickering rays of sun. The sight of those sinewed forearms made her tummy dip and roll. "It went better than expected."

"Nikandros, what—"

He pushed off from the wall, an edginess to his movements. "I need to get out of here, at least for a while," he said, cutting her off. Dismissing her.

"Here, where?"

"The palace. Andreas. Everything remotely connected to this…place."

Her heart sank. She didn't want him to leave again. But more than that, she didn't want him to shut her out just when they were taking tentative steps toward each other. And if something was happening between him and Andreas, if something was upsetting him, she wanted to understand and help. The depth of her need to comfort him shook her. "When will you return?"

"I don't know."

She reached for the ends of his undone tie and stalled him when he'd have walked by her.

Blue-black hair glinting, his body grazing her side, he stilled. That arrogant head bent toward her shoulder. The scent of him, male skin and sweat, stroked her in tantalizing waves and her heart began to beat faster. The strength and breadth of his powerful body—Mia wanted to nuzzle into him and stay there forever.

And in his current mood, he'd oblige her. He held her hips in a grip that screamed possession and sexual need, but there was no seduction or laughter in it. None of that raw honesty that colored every word and movement of his.

When she tried to nudge out of his hold, he tightened his grip, a raspy growl emanating from his throat. An answering thrum vibrated within Mia. He was faintly shaking with anger or whatever held him in thrall. And she wasn't going to let him walk away if her life depended on it.

"Nikandros, where are you going and when will you return?" she said loudly in the sizzling silence, enunciating each word as if he were a child.

His teeth bared against the bare skin of her upper arm, scraped at her skin. Mia jerked, a bolt of sensation arrowing down to the place between her thighs. Awareness thickened around them.

"I don't know where I'm going and I don't know when I will return," he replied in that same tone.

"That's not good enough," she said, holding the silk tight.

He lifted his brow in a sardonic tilt. "For a woman who doesn't want to be *tied* to me in any way, you do a very good pretense of a clingy girlfriend or even a wife, *pethi mou*." The blue rings of his eyes glittered close, a hardness tightening his mouth. "I hate people who go in half measures. How you ever won a game of soccer when all you do is stand on the sidelines is a wonder to me."

Mia blinked, his words piercing deep and sharp. No retort came because he was right. It was only on the soccer field that she'd never held back, where she'd felt fearless and alive.

Only to soccer that she'd ever completely given herself.

He looked just like Brian had done when she'd asked for a divorce that night. Even as fear flew in her veins, Mia swallowed that memory back. The last thing she wanted was to throw Brian's name into the mix right now.

"I don't care what you think I'm acting like, but you can't leave this room until you calm down. I won't let you go off half-cocked on some crazy mountainous drive or jump from the sky, just because you want to get control over the situation."

"No?"

"No."

"You think that's what I usually do? Throw myself at the mercy of nature because I'm mad at something?" A small smile flitted across his mouth. "I'd have definitely ended up with broken limbs in some crevice."

"It's not funny," she said, jerking the tie in her hands. "I still won't let you go."

He tucked one damp lock of hair away from her forehead, his whisper a caress against the rim of her ear. "There's a sure way of calming me down." Air depleted from the vicinity, his hard body grazing her hip like a sinuous caress. His hand slipped under her thin T-shirt and found the ridge of her spine. Up and down, he traced a finger, sneaking in under her sports bra and teasing the rim of her low-slung shorts. "I want hard, furious sex, Mia. I want to be inside you."

Mia thought she'd melt from within. His erection nudged at the curve of her hip. Need filled her so fast and so thickly that she stood like that.

"Sex is not communication," she finally said.

Devilish blue eyes glimmered. "Who said anything about communication?"

"If you want to get out of here—" neither mind-blowing sex nor letting Nikandros walk away from her was an option "—fine. Give me ten minutes and I'll be ready."

Something glittered in his eyes but he didn't push her. "And where shall we go while we wait for Andreas to decide?"

"I've been here close to four weeks and you've shown me nothing of Drakon. I want to go on a date," she said, saying the first thing that came to her mind.

"A date?" he asked, disbelief pinching his brows.

"Why do you look so shocked?"

"It's the first time you've willingly mentioned, much less suggested a course of action about us."

"Maybe I'm getting used to this…thing between us. That you and I, can, against all odds, work."

He laughed. The flash of his even white teeth, the way it banished the shadows from his eyes, her breath left her in a gush of relief. "You're so good for my ego, *pethi mou*."

Rolling her eyes at his sarcasm, Mia tried to sift through her own emotions. He was right. Again, the blasted man. But this felt good. Asserting this control over her and Nik and the course of their life felt exhilarating.

Wanting to know and comfort him came more naturally than anything had in a long time. "Our relationship is all jumbled up with twisted history, like you said. And to complicate it, we somehow ended up starting with sex and—" a lascivious grin curved his mouth at that and Mia batted his finger away from her neck "—and now we're going to have a child. And I say, let's do one thing conventionally.

"Take me out today. Spend the rest of it with me."

He gave her an assessing look. "You're serious?"

"I've never been more serious about anything in my life."

Maybe it was the challenge in her tone. Or the demand in it. But a flicker of warmth shone through the hardness in his expression. "You're on, *pethi mou.*"

While Mia digested the consequences of her actions, he undid the rest of the buttons and pulled his shirt off. Then his nimble fingers went to his trousers.

Heat flaring like little pockets on her skin, Mia watched as he tugged the zipper down. The sight of the sculpted V of his groin was an electric shock that spurred her into action. To halt him, she closed her hand over his.

His erection twitched under her hand, a loud hiss falling from his lips.

Dear God, he was so big and he'd been inside her. He'd made such pleasure revel through her. Heat poured from his hardness into her palm, burning her to the core. He nuzzled into the crook of her neck while his hips thrust into her palm. "Damn it all to hell, Mia, you've got to at least give me—"

Something he'd said clicked in the lust-soaked recesses of her mind. Mia jerked her hand away and clasped his cheeks. Darkened blue eyes ate her up. "What is Andreas deciding, Nikandros?"

And just like that, every inch of warmth disappeared

from his face. "Whether he can truly give up the ropes or not. Whether he wants me here or not."

"Here, where? In the palace? Are you thinking of moving somewhere else in Drakon?"

Dark emotion flared in his eyes. "No, he has to decide whether he wants me in Drakon at all. Andreas has to decide if he trusts me, if he's willing to take a risk with me, if he can put Drakon's economy in my hands. As I expected, the dear Crown Prince still hasn't learned that it's all or nothing with me." He said that so casually that it took Mia a couple of minutes to understand him. "A concept people seem to find incredibly hard to grasp."

"And if he doesn't give you carte blanche on Drakon's economy?"

He didn't answer but the hard line of his mouth said more than he needed to.

His trousers hanging over the lean curve of his hips, revealing the line of dark hair that disappeared into the seam of his boxers, he said, "The chopper will leave in twenty minutes."

In the dangerous mood he seemed to be currently in, he would leave without her. And she was not at all prepared to be left behind by Nikandros Drakos anywhere.

Not anymore.

He needed her, even if he was too thickheaded and arrogant to see it. Even if he'd rather coat that need in the guise of sex.

And Nikandros needing her, for sex and anything else, was a drug that seemed to fizz through Mia's veins. Until she couldn't even recognize the woman staring at her with big eyes and trembling mouth in the damp mirror.

She had blurted out the first thing that came to her mind, but God, she felt as if she was sixteen. And she was going out on a date with the Prince she'd made googly eyes over from afar.

CHAPTER EIGHT

MIA SHOULD HAVE known that a helicopter tour of Drakon with Nikandros meant that Nikandros would be the one piloting it. He had, however, inquired if she was allowed to go on such a trip in her current condition, and when she'd stared at him blankly, assured her that he wouldn't take any risks.

And so Mia got her first sight of sky-kissed mountains and white beaches with Nikandros's expert commentary right in her ear. It was a tour unlike any she'd have gotten if she'd visited as a tourist.

Nikandros spiced up his descriptions with ancient stories of warriors and feuds, colorful and almost unbelievable tales of dragons and treasures. But with every word he said, every tale he told with relish, one thing stood out for Mia.

Drakon was an integral part of him, its history, from its mountainous ranges to the villages struggling to build a sustainable economy—it was all in his blood. A rich heritage that would one day be her child's too.

And the dark shadow of leaving it again didn't leave

those blue eyes even as he entertained her with such great stories.

He had walked away once. And whatever Andreas was doing today, a part of Nikandros would be ripped from him if he left Drakon again.

He knew of all the backwater cafés and lovely spots that no visitor would ever trample.

They had lunch at a seafood place that reminded Mia of a restaurant back home in Miami. Wherever they went, people recognized him, though most kept a respectful distance too.

But even without the mantle of being their Prince, he attracted attention wherever they went. A startlingly gorgeous man, he turned women's heads every time he moved. His attention, however, hadn't wavered from Mia for a single minute.

It was quite possibly the best day Mia had had in a long time.

After lunch, he brought them to a private strip of white sandy beach. The turquoise water surrounded by groves of trees and rocky coves was a slice of paradise. Rolling up his jeans, Nik joined Mia as she waded into the ice-cold water. Finally, they settled on a nice shady spot a little inland, a comfortable silence settling between them.

Mia thought he would kiss her on the deserted beach, if not seduce her, but he did nothing of the sort, even though that flare of awareness between them hadn't dimmed one bit.

"Tell me what's going on with the investors."

She thought he would brush her off again, tell her it

was none of her business. Instead, he sighed and looked at her. The blue of the ocean had nothing on the ice blue of Nikandros's eyes. "Then you'll have to hear about all the dirty past. About what I'm capable of. Things I have done—"

"You think I haven't done things I regret? Things that come back to haunt me every day?" She gripped the warm white sand in her hand, as tight and hard as she could.

But the second her fingers twitched, the sand fell through.

So much time wasted, so many regrets. Tears scratched her throat but she held them off. "Things I wish I could take back."

Their shadows separated their bodies and Mia wondered when he'd pulled away from her.

"I seduced the woman Andreas was officially betrothed to," Nikandros said, not for shock value but because he knew, with her history with Brian, that was the part that would disgust Mia.

Almost a decade later, it disgusted him still.

She stared at him, shock parting her lips. "You did what?"

Nik thrust his hands through his hair roughly, a sort of edginess creeping into him at the thought of that time. "You have to understand the twisted dysfunctional dynamic between Theos and Andreas and me...to comprehend how much I hate being back in the palace.

"For most of my life, my father ignored me, except inquiring every once in a while if his spare was going to make it."

"Make it?" she said with a distaste that she couldn't get rid of.

Nikandros shrugged. "Theos hated that I was useless to him. Took it as a personal insult that one of *his offspring* could be such a sick child.

"He had only time for Andreas—he was obsessed with turning him into the perfect heir. When I remember all the stories they told about his training regimen for Andreas…it's clear now Theos possessed the streak of madness even then.

"The result is Andreas and I never knew each other. I hero-worshipped him because I grew up listening to tales of the Crown Prince but he…never had any time for me.

"The year I turned nineteen, my health improved. No fainting spells, no blighted fevers, no recurring pneumonia. No watching the world from the prison of my apartments, wishing I could laugh and play and just…live."

Mia's chest hurt at the ache she heard in his voice. It was impossible to imagine this vital man as a sick child and, even worse, the longing of a boy to join his brother.

"Suddenly, the entire world was mine for the taking. My mother begged me to leave with her, to travel and see the world. She tried to get me to leave Drakon at any cost. But…for so long, I'd wanted to be my father's son and Prince of Drakon.

"And Theos…he took me under his wing.

"I wanted to join the army, but he said no. University, no. Travel the world, no. But I didn't care because he was spending all this time with me. Andreas, he said, was taking time away from the palace for the moment. Which should have made all kinds of red flags go up for me.

"Suddenly, I was his favorite son. Slowly, he started pulling my strings, like he'd done for so long with Andreas and I chafed.

"And then I met Isabella Marquez. She and a friend of hers were summering in Drakon and I fell violently in love with her."

"Violently?" Mia looked like she was nauseated.

"Is there a different kind when you're twenty and realize you're not going to die as predicted?" Just talking about that period of his life made his skin crawl. "We sneaked into nightclubs, we went skiing, we partied into all hours with her friends.

"During this time, Theos realized I wasn't as malleable as Andreas. Still, he tried. *Christos*, every time there was a public appearance, he read me the riot act on protocol. Security, decorum, conventions to be followed, the unlimited number of people who ran my life, who told me how to sit, stand, look at someone… it became unbearable.

"It was as if I had transferred from one cage at the hospital to another. With even less freedom. And then Andreas returned, and overnight everything changed."

Eyes big in her face, Mia whispered, "What happened?"

"Apparently, Andreas and my father had been locking horns for the past few months. He'd even talked of giving up the throne. But whatever had happened, by the time I had realized my father had only been using me, the matter between them was resolved.

"The Crown Prince was back in every sense of the word, even more uptight and rigid than before. Theos shoved me aside. He said he was sick and tired of trying to pass off the runt as a purebred. That I had to come to scratch if I was to be Prince of Drakon."

A self-deprecating smile curved his mouth. Slowly, all the things she'd seen since she'd arrived in Drakon made sense to Mia.

She couldn't believe how Nik could speak in that dry tone. Couldn't imagine how keenly that rejection would have scarred a young man. "That's awful, Nik. My parents loved me and Emmanuela the same. To be so ghastly to your own child…"

"All my life I craved Theos's attention only to realize what a chokehold it was. I was ready to carve out my own path by then. I told Theos I was done with him.

"And Theos announced that Isabella and Andreas were to be betrothed, that he and her brother had been working out details of an alliance all this while. I couldn't believe Isabella had known about it."

A soft gasp left Mia's mouth and she cringed at what was coming. "Please tell me you told Andreas what she meant to you." Her words were a whisper against the sound of crashing waves, against the sound of the dark bitterness that seemed to engulf Nikandros.

"I begged him to refuse the alliance, to defy my father's plans for once. My brother showed as much understanding as the pile of rocks he lives on. He said no woman would choose the spare when she could have the Crown Prince.

"I spent the night full of vitriol, hating him, calling him a thousand foolish names.

"The next week, I went to Isabella and asked her to run away with me. She said while it had been fun and she cared for me, I'd only been a distraction. And I could offer her nothing in comparison to the status of being the next queen of Drakon.

"I could have walked away at that point, *ne*? Let them all go to hell. But I seduced her again, and weak as she was, she gave in." Distaste colored his words, his gaze haunted. "In the early hours of dawn, drunk and raving, I sought Andreas and told him I'd taken his future bride's virginity long ago. That for once, he'd know what it felt to come second.

"He stood there and stared at me, and then in that deep voice of his, asked me if I wanted assistance to get to my suite.

"I woke up hungover and disgusted with myself.

"Fighting with Theos, resenting Andreas for everything he was and I was not... I couldn't face what I became between those walls. Isabella and Andreas and my father taught me an invaluable lesson, stripped the blinders from the naive youth I'd been."

Swallowing the ache in the back of her throat, Mia asked the question she desperately didn't want an answer to—what was the lesson? Suddenly, she felt as if she were standing outside a solid door behind which lay Nikandros's heart. "That to care about anyone is to give them power over me, to let them decide what I'm worth.

"And I've fought for life too much for that to be decided by anyone else.

"I left Drakon two days later."

Mia's throat felt parched. She couldn't even process the scars his past must have left on him. Still, he hadn't dwelled in the past. He'd lived life by his own rules.

What is left when you run from yourself, he'd asked her that day. Because, he'd found that, despite everything, his brother and father had had a place in his life still.

"But you still came back. You've forgiven each other. Why would Andreas want you to leave now?"

"The investor I found for Drakon's new economy, the company belongs to Gabriel Marquez."

"Jesus, Isabella's brother?"

"Yes. Gabriel is renowned for his ruthless investments. He wants a piece of Drakon and he and I together can change the way the world sees us. But, of course, Andreas is smarting at giving up the reins. Tax reform, new banking policies, he recited a hundred obstacles to my face, but it's clear what the problem is."

Mia was only half listening, all her thoughts on the woman. Nikandros had been in love with Isabella. Had she utterly broken his heart? How could he ever trust again when she'd made him doubt his very identity? When she'd shoved him aside as easily as his father had done? "What happened to Ms. Marquez?"

"She married a member of the extended branch of the Dutch royal family. She got what she wanted. And Gabriel pulled his company out of the huge deal father had been about to make with him."

"And you don't understand Andreas's concern? You…might have ruined his sister's life, together. Why take a risk in inviting such a man into Drakon? I don't understand anything of investments and economies, and even to me, it seems like it's full of risks.

"Christ, Nik. Couldn't you have found a different investor?"

With a sudden movement, he stood up and reached out a hand to her. "I trust that Gabriel is ready to let bygones be bygones. Andreas should trust my judgment."

"After you both trampled it so thoroughly between yourselves? When you admit that Andreas and you never even had a chance to learn each other?

"Trust has to be earned, Nikandros."

His head reared back, as if she had struck him. A shutter fell over his eyes, pushing Mia away, as violently as if he'd slammed a door in her face. "No!

"Trust is given freely. Trust is not a set of calculations you use to make a decision. It's a gut instinct. Don't tell me you never made a call on the field in the middle of a game based on what your gut said and not statistics or a player's technique.

"Andreas needs to trust that I would not do anything that would jeopardize Drakon. That it is a part of me as much as it is of him. That I…know what I'm talking about.

"He either gives me this chance or he doesn't. I will not play in the parameters he sets for me as if I were another member of his bloody staff. As if I were his puppet.

"Just as I will not wait forever for you to make a decision, Mia.

"Do not mistake my patience to be my weakness.

We marry or we face each other in a custody battle in the court and in the media. But I won't let anyone take away what should be mine ever again.

"Not you and not Andreas."

Mia was on tenterhooks all through the next two days, as Nikandros waited for Andreas's decision. Nikandros's drive to turn around Drakon's economy, to have a place in Drakon after all these years—it was another side of him she'd never expected.

It was as if being back in the palace had brought out his ruthlessness. But even she couldn't shrug off the history seeped in the palace walls, the isolation Nikandros must have felt when, again and again, he'd been told he didn't measure up in ways he couldn't control.

The Crown Prince had been holed up in discussions with his financial advisors and members of the Crown Council, all of whom were against changing the decades-old investment policy in Drakon. The last bit of information had been supplied by Eleni when Mia had pestered her about it.

Not only was Marquez Holdings Inc. reputed to be ruthless in taking hold of international markets, but the highest criticism of the corporation was that it had taken over controlling interest of the companies it had saved from the brink of disaster. In Nik's defense—Mia had stayed up reading up everything she could—neither had MHI ever lost on a risk it had made.

Nikandros, however, didn't join Andreas in any of those meetings, even though he'd been invited to. Neither did he seek her out again in the following days.

He closeted himself in his office for hours on end, she knew, making alternative plans. His frustration and fury, it was a wall she couldn't scale between them.

She knew that he was consumed by this stillness that Andreas had brought him to, but the few times they looked at each other, she also sensed his retreat from her.

A polite distance in his smile, a cool, almost stranger-like quality in his gaze made her long for his open, even if sometimes eviscerating, honesty.

Strangely, she was not worried about losing their child to him in a custody battle as much as she was of losing him.

There were so many things Mia understood about him now.

Why he'd been determined to be a part of their child's life, the fury in his eyes when she'd dismissed him as a sperm donor, his hair-raising lifestyle...

No one had ever believed in him all his life.

Not his father then and not his brother now, it would seem.

And yet, even after the treatment he'd received at the hands of them both, even after he'd spent so much of his life isolated from everyone, he had come back to Drakon.

Giving Andreas a chance. Giving his father a chance.

And maybe giving Mia a chance too. Whether any of them deserved it or not.

He'd made a huge commitment to her.

She also understood only now that he made it without any emotional attachment to her. If it weren't for their unborn child, Nikandros wouldn't have given her another thought. Any woman he'd tangled with—he would treat the same way.

He'd shower them with gifts, he'd give them time or whatever the hell they asked for, and in return, he'd expect the same commitment.

For all his defiance of conventions, Nikandros at his core was very much a traditional man. He believed in family, and friendships, everything that tied people together.

But his heart—would she ever have a place in it? Or had they all trampled the generous heart of that vulnerable twenty-year-old he'd been? Had that woman forever stolen his ability to love?

Suddenly, that Nikandros had been forced to choose her because of her pregnancy sat like a thorn under her skin.

Seeing him walking around the courtyard of the palace from their bedroom, Mia felt an ache like she'd never known. It was a sharp, powerless beat in her chest to do something to make it right for him.

To be something more to him than the woman who carried his child.

Ignoring the protocol Eleni had been drilling into her for weeks now, Mia knocked and entered the office of the man she had taken an instant dislike to from that first lunch.

Andreas was seated behind a huge mahogany desk, the sheer, polished sheen of it fading in contrast to his richly dark olive skin.

No man hid behind that cool reserve and arrogance

better than the Crown Prince of Drakon. The pain in
Nik's eyes as he'd told her what Andreas had said and
what he'd driven Nik to all those years ago—she wondered if there was truly nothing behind that facade.

"What have you decided?" she asked without pre-
amble. She heard Eleni gasp, saw two of his aides jerk
their heads in her direction. She didn't give a damn.

His gaze took her in, and with a nod, he dispatched
all of them, including his sister. If he'd felt any surprise
at her barging into his office when she avoided him at
every cost usually, he didn't show it.

"Good afternoon, Mrs. Morgan."

"I wish I could say the same, Your Highness," she
said. He didn't quite smile but there was a gleam of
something in those unblinking eyes. "I want to know
your decision."

Pushing away from the desk, he walked around it.
"About what?"

Power vibrated around him, making her wonder
again if there was anything else to him. "About Marquez Holdings Inc. investing in Drakon."

"It has nothing to do with you. Not a stretch to even
say it's a highly confidential state matter at this point.
You…have no *status* with my brother, Mrs. Morgan. For
some reason that I don't fathom, Nik is giving you time.
But then, he's always been the kinder one between us.

"In the scheme of Drakon and its future, you're, right
now, inconsequential."

Mia was aware he was riling her, but anger bubbled
over anyway. The pain in Nik's eyes scraped at that
anger. "My daughter or son is the next generation of

your bloody country. I'm going to be Nikandros's wife so I have every right to know what kind of game you're playing this time."

"Does my brother know that you've decided to marry him then?" he inquired silkily.

Mia clutched the back of a dark leather seat, only now realizing what she'd betrayed. When had she decided to marry Nikandros? How had he stolen under her defenses so well?

As long as it was a commitment they both could honor for their child, as long as she didn't pin all her hopes and dreams on a man who craved challenge in every aspect of his life, she could take this step. She could build a life with him.

But the warning didn't calm the panic spiraling through her.

"I care about making sure Nikandros does not feel alone when you betray him."

"Betrayal? That sounds very dramatic, Mrs. Morgan."

"No, I don't think so. Because I'm beginning to put things together. You made sure to tell Nik that I was pregnant. You leaked the news to the press giving Nik and I no choice but to reconcile to it. And then you dangled a new challenge in front of Nikandros and hooked him. All for what?"

"Really, Mrs.—"

"Jesus, Andreas, enough!" Mia was more shocked than him at her raised voice. "What the hell do you truly want? What is this, revenge for what he did with Isabella?"

"Nikandros belongs in Drakon."

It was the first thing the arrogant Prince had ever said that Mia completely agreed with.

She dug her fingers into the soft leather. "Then why the hell can't you keep your word? Why are you doubting him now? Will you ruin what little happiness he hopes to gain now?"

"And does his happiness matter so much to you, Mrs. Morgan? Now that he's decided to be Prince of Drakon again?"

A cold chill poured down Mia's spine. "Nik is right. You are truly your father's son. He should cut his losses with you, with this bloody country. And I'm going to—"

If Mia's ire hadn't been so focused on him, she'd have missed his flinch.

"I know my brother better than anyone else," he finally said after so long that Mia thought she was imagining his deep voice in the thick silence. "Still, I didn't realize how much my...how much Drakon consumes him.

"Whatever I do today... I will lose him, Mia. And I have lost much already."

His tone unsettled Mia to the core of her being. But she had committed herself to this path now. To Nikandros and their child, and this time, she'd do anything to make it work. And she'd take on anyone for him. That fierceness ran rampant in her veins. "You think to corral him while keeping him in Drakon?

"Be careful, Andreas. If he decides he doesn't want this enough, you'll never get another chance."

"My father's hold on us, it's... I only want the best for him."

As she walked away from the Crown Prince, Mia knew without doubt that she didn't want to spend the rest of her life without Nikandros in it. She wanted to marry him. She wanted to raise their child along with him. She wanted to be the woman he chose because he needed her, not because of the accident of their child.

She was damned if she lost this...before she had even started playing. But she was nervous as hell too, because after soccer, she'd never wanted anything this desperately.

CHAPTER NINE

Days blurred into weeks and got longer as spring slowly gave way to summer. Nikandros had forgotten how much he liked the long summer days in Drakon, how the very city seemed to come alive. But he'd barely taken notice of any of it after Andreas agreed to change the investment policy that had dictated Drakon's economy for decades.

Giving the reins of it to Nikandros.

He had no room to breathe once he had set the wheels in motion to sign a deal with Marquez Holdings Inc. to invest in Drakon. He'd had flown out to see Gabriel in Barcelona two more times. Continuous talks were being held with financial advisors and cabinet members to forge new tax laws for companies that invested in the country.

As ruthless as Gabriel was, Nikandros had the fierce satisfaction of dictating his own terms.

In another week or two, Gabriel and his team would move to Drakon for the initial scouting. No project he'd ever taken on consumed Nikandros's attention quite like this new venture.

His office had been inundated with visits from members of cabinet to the Crown Council, some to greet him, some to take his measure. Some to make bets on whether Andreas had signed off on Drakon's ruination by giving him power over the country's portfolio.

By the time one week merged into the next, invitations to royal balls and garden parties, from all the power players in their small municipality had stacked up.

He had to pick an administrative assistant, a social secretary, a PR aide—staff completely unnecessary to his actual work.

From how he looked to what he wore to who he was going to talk to and what he was going to say to them, everything was a state-level decision that had him spewing obscenities. If one more old-timer reminded him that King Theos did it this way or that the Crown Prince always took the traditional way, he was going to explode.

Within two weeks, Nikandros was already smarting at the confines of decorum and diplomacy, whereas Andreas had spent all of his life, since he'd been a boy, mired in this. With no one to even share his thoughts with except Theos, who had been power mad and obsessed with Drakon's security. For the first time in his life, Nikandros had a small glimpse into what life had been for his brother.

To the growing unease of most of his advisors and staff, he damned decorum and protocol when it got in the way of getting things done.

Life changed at a rapid pace for Nik and not just on the work front. If he was a man with a mission, it seemed Mia had one of her own, though what it was he had no idea.

The one thing he knew was that there was something different about her. She was coming into her own with Eleni and Andreas, he realized as he watched her easily put his brother and sister in place when they interfered. He caught her looking at him more than once, her perusal thorough and lacking artifice in a way that always told him she was looking at him.

But all they'd traded were polite exchanges—he inquired after her health and she about his work. He'd even taken to avoiding their suite until after midnight.

The stubborn woman still slept on the chaise, determined to push him to the very last thread of his control. If he had to spend the rest of his life carting her off to his bed, he would do it. Except it was only getting harder and harder to walk toward his cold shower.

Especially when Mia had the habit of tucking up against his side while asleep. Sweat beading his brow, he'd been more than tempted to take that lush mouth, to drift his hand down her alluring curves. She wanted him as much as he wanted her; he could so easily seduce her. But he didn't want her like that.

She hadn't bristled at the ultimatum he'd given her on the beach that day. Not called him a ruthless bastard as he deserved to be. Simply congratulated him the night when Andreas announced that he was opening Drakon's economy.

He'd been so angry with Andreas, frustrated with being thwarted at every action he took, yes. But threatening Mia, who'd done nothing but anchor him that day, with a custody battle, it was a low he never wanted to sink to again.

It was far too reminiscent of tactics his father had used on him and Andreas. It smacked too much of losing control, of becoming that weak man who'd seduce a woman betrothed to his brother just to prove he could.

So for the first time in his life, he'd avoided Mia. He needed distance and perspective. Straddling the fine line between Gabriel's risk-laden strategies and Andreas's conventional wisdom was a challenge that took all the perspective he could summon.

And luckily, for him, focusing on something to the exclusion of everything else came very easily.

The twelfth strike of the clock bore into his thoughts when Nikandros stood up from his desk after another long day and found Mia standing at the open door. In a white cover-up that fell to her toned thighs and left a deep V at her chest, giving him a hint of the valley beneath.

Lust was a visceral punch to his gut as he stared at her. Other concerns followed soon after. "Mia, what is it? Are you unwell?"

"I haven't seen you all this week, Nikandros."

"I have been busy."

"I know. I just thought you might join me for a swim. And we can spend some time together."

He raised a brow and she flushed. "You've been avoiding me. I thought once Andreas settled things, you'd relax. Unless you've changed your mind about marrying me, you can't avoid me forever, Nik."

Nikandros pushed a hand through his hair. She was

right. "I have been postponing having to apologize to you."

"For what?"

"For breaking my word and throwing that outrageous threat at you about custody."

"Knowing how angry you were, I didn't give it any credit. From the beginning, I think I always trusted your intentions, Nikandros. It's what happens when we both mix that scares me."

"It's been a long, dry spell but I have vague memories of that night, and I'd say what happens when we mix is fantastic, Mia."

Eyes wide, she fought the curve of her mouth. But eventually, her smile broke through. "So, will you join me in that swim or what?"

Suddenly, nothing was more inviting than a midnight swim and tormenting Mia as she did him.

The water was cold and crisp, but not icy.

In black swimming trunks, he was cutting through the water with long strokes when Mia took off her wrap and made a smooth dive into the water.

In an orange two-piece bikini. Three triangles at the top and two at the bottom that made his breath hitch in the water.

Slender shoulders rising over the water, she raised a brow when he stared at her soundlessly. An impish smile followed. The minx knew how stunning and sexy she looked in those orange scraps.

Was she taunting him on purpose? That this was probably Mia's way of communicating that she was ready for things to go forward between them filled his blood with a heated rush.

She was a graceful swimmer, easily matching his stride in the water in an unspoken challenge. He felt her gaze on him, almost a caress.

They swam in silence for a while, the velvety darkness of the night punctured by the meager light from the path. The scent of jasmine was heavy here, coating the air with its fragrance. The night seemed to have come to a standstill along with them, waiting and watching with a pregnant expectation.

When she reached one edge of the pool and floated on her back there, he joined her. "Tell me why the midnight swim." He'd meant to make it a gentle question. Instead it came out as a possessive command.

Sleek limbs gleaming golden in the moonlight, she sighed. "No one's ever asked me about that."

He wanted to know. He wanted parts of her no one had ever known. "Not even Brian?"

She looked at him then, as though reminding him that he was breaking his own rule. "No. Although I don't think I'd have told him even if he'd asked."

"Why not?"

"He'd have sold it to some tabloid, or sports magazine. Put a PR spin on it. This is far too private for me."

"It is something I've always wondered about," he said, thinking of those early days when he'd met her. He'd been twenty then, and she seventeen. She'd been like a bullet on the field, full of laughter and energy. And shy and reticent off it. "Before I could ask you, you were dating Brian, and then married him.

"After that, it became imperative that the less I indulged my interest in you, the better. I think it became easier to believe everything Brian said about you and your marriage in the face of my obsession with you, Mia."

She flipped with a grace that fascinated him and swam to the edge of the pool. Water droplets followed the long indent of her spine and all he wanted to do was follow the trail with his tongue. The dip of her waist, the flare of her hips, the lush curves of her buttocks, there wasn't an inch that wasn't perfection.

She turned to face him, and the swell of her breasts floated above the water. Hair plastered to her face, her features were starkly beautiful, the same reserved cast to them.

But tonight, Nik saw more, beyond that reserve. He saw the same loneliness he'd glimpsed in his own eyes when he looked at the mirror, the same restlessness. He saw an innate shyness.

She'd loved soccer, not the glamour that had surrounded the world. Neither the extravagant, flamboyant lifestyle that Brian had dragged her into.

Christos, they couldn't have been more mismatched. "Why did you marry him?"

"You know, I've been wondering the same thing the last few weeks. I never thought about it before."

He waited. Pulling himself out of the pool, he extended a hand to her. Once she was out, he grabbed a towel and covered her.

When she stiffened in his arms, he wrapped them

around her loosely. It was unbearable to be near her and not touch her.

"He was the only one who asked me," she said with a soft smile. "I accepted because he was a safe bet. The Brian I went out with was hardworking, affectionate, and with not a bad habit or weakness in sight." She scoffed, a jeering mockery that seemed to pain her. "Then his career took off and he began to be obsessed with his own celebrity. High stakes poker games, racing circuits, souped-up vehicles, he threw money at everything. He worshipped you." When he'd have interrupted, she said, "No. You don't have to say it. I realized two days after I came here that you and he are nothing alike."

"Mia, you don't have to talk about this."

"No, I do. The risks he took, his spending habits, what he did was so reminiscent of my father...that I instantly froze him out. I couldn't bear to be hurt like that again.

"I retreated and he was incapable of reaching me. He cheated until it was all one vicious spiral.

"So, you see, you were right, I was partly responsible. But his death... God, I never wanted him to die, Nik. I..."

Nikandros held her tighter, feeling powerless against the grief shaking her. To think he'd said those horrible things to her... "It's okay, *agape mou.*"

Instantly, her tension rose, her pulse flickering madly in her neck. "Shh..." he whispered, gently landing his fingers on her shoulders. "I just want to hold you, Mia." Taking another towel, Nikandros slowly wiped at her dripping hair.

She stiffened and his hands eased. Continuing the soft movements, he replaced the towel with his fingers and combed out the damp silky locks.

Her exhale came in a rush and slowly the line of her spine settled against his chest. There was nothing sexual about his touch, and yet, he felt her struggling to relax. Struggling to reach out to him.

Only then did Nikandros realize what it must have cost her to come to him tonight. "You will nuzzle into me in sleep. You'll cling to me in a nightmare. You will slap me because you're terrified I'll kill myself. And *Christos*, you'll face the ruthless tyrant that is Andreas on my behalf." A sharp ache twisted deep in his belly at the reminder of what Eleni had told him today. At all the efforts Mia had been making to fit into her new life. Mia was no longer in limbo, his sister had said, no longer resistant to her role in Drakon. "And yet, you can't admit that you want this...between us."

"I've been yours for the taking since that night. God, Nik, what else do you want from me?"

"I need to hear you say it. Not just the sex but this relationship. What is it about us that scares you so much?"

"I don't know how to handle small things like attraction and men and you...you're not even normal."

He pulled her to him, their breaths choppy in the silence. "What?"

"You're gorgeous, charming, a bloody prince, for God's sake. I'm way out of my depth."

"You were a world-class champion. I idolized you on the soccer field and obsessed about you when you were off it," he said easily. "How much more power could you want over me?"

"Intimacy is hard for me. I spent my teenage years training long hours. What little time I had, I spent studying. The only man I ever truly loved was my father, and he broke my heart over and over until I... Opening myself to you, letting myself care about this... it terrifies me, Nik."

"Then let me understand. Let me help you as you've helped me."

She slowly relaxed in his hold, her hands sitting on top of his. "My father was the American Dream come true. When they were mere kids, he and my mother immigrated from Mexico City and started this small café that eventually grew to three restaurants." Pride resonated in her voice. "But as long as I can remember, he had a gambling habit. That high when he won would be glorious and when he lost..."

The pain in her tone had Nik tightening his arms around her. "Did he hurt you? Or your mother?"

"No, God, never." She shook her head violently, spraying him with water. "He was a good man, Nik. A wonderful husband, a loving father to me and Emmanuela. Used to call us his little champions.

"But see, it wasn't enough, not when he was in the grip of that urge, not when he was chasing that high.

"Each year, he got progressively worse until he started gambling away every little thing we owned. In those last few years, he rarely even came home from the club. Stopped taking me to soccer practice.

"He was the one who got me into it—my biggest supporter and my fan.

"With heavy gambling losses of course came drinking. My mother would drive to the club every evening to bring him home. I always went along because I missed him terribly.

"The groundskeeper at the club—he was a man my dad had helped out long ago. One day, he asked me if I wanted to swim while I waited.

"I had already started playing soccer at the local club and I needed all the exercise I could get. I think, for almost three years, we went to that club every night and I swam while my mother tried to convince him to finish for the night.

"Slowly we lost everything.

"High school came and went. When a scout asked me if I was interested in playing on the junior team at Miami, I left and never looked back."

"Never looked back?"

She flinched, as if it was the one thing she didn't want to talk about. "My mother begged me to not leave then. She said it would crush my dad to see me walk away. To see me give up on him.

"But what about all the hopes I'd built around him? What about all the thousands of times he'd promised me he'd give it up only to crush them again and again?

"I had a huge argument with her. I said horrible things. That soccer was more important to me than a gambling addict. That she should leave him too. God, I was so horrible to my own parents. So angry and scared…"

"You were sixteen, Mia. All of us have been there."

"After I found some success, I sent money through my sister. But I don't think Mom ever forgave me for speaking like that about him. For walking away.

"But, I couldn't stay anymore, Nik. I couldn't bear to watch him like that."

Words are so easy, she'd said that night. *Actions speak louder.* And then Brian had gone the same way.

He understood her fear now.

She thought Nik would break all the promises he made, too. That if she trusted him, he would only crush her. Such a fragile heart she hid under that resilience.

Was it any wonder she refused to trust him, to open herself up? The smallest of wounds from childhood left deep scars. He should know. He couldn't blame her for guarding her heart.

"Your father, how is he now?"

Her tears fell on his wrists. "He passed away three years after I left. I didn't even make it to the funeral because I was on the championship tour. I've never been able to sleep before midnight, so I swim."

"Come here, *matia mou*," he whispered, folding his arms around her trembling body. Nuzzling into his chest, she came to him without a word. The rush of tenderness Nik felt disarmed him.

He wished he could do something, anything to fix this for her. He held her like that for how long he didn't know but the dark night stilled around them.

Hardening his heart, he pressed a kiss to her temple. "I understand now how hard it is for you to—"

She wrapped her hands around his neck, pushing herself onto her toes. "I do trust you, Nikandros. I want to put everything I have into making this work. But opening myself up to you will take—"

Nikandros didn't let her finish. He shifted down and nuzzled at her top lip. When she gasped, he pressed ahead, a faint drumming in his ears. He only meant to seal her promise with a kiss but in mere seconds, the kiss took on a life of its own.

Her soft breath hit his jaw like a caress, her breasts plastered to his chest sending deep shivers of need through him.

This was right too, some primal instinct reared inside him. Mia and he were right. The sound of a throat clearing, again and again, filtered through the lust soaking his mind. Mia hid her face in his chest, her body trembling in his arms.

"Your Highness?"

Nikandros had to swallow a couple of times to find his voice. Of all the times—damn it all to hell. If it was Andreas summoning him, he would commit fratricide.

An aide materialized at the pool's side, a dark shadow in the moonlight. His face landed somewhere near Nik's head. "The Crown Prince has summoned you, Your Highness. Your father... I was told to inform you that King Theos is slipping away. And he asks for you incessantly."

It was almost as if King Theos knew that his sons were forging a bond with each other.

Mia had no idea what was said between him and his sons. But the worse the news about his deteriorating health, the edgier Nikandros seemed to get. And Andreas too. It was as if that placid calm was beginning to fray at the edges.

Nikandros worked with Gabriel's team at nothing short of an inhuman pace, with no time for anyone. Andreas's warning began to beat a tattoo inside her head.

Mia had been so worried about both of them that she'd mentioned the idea of a friendly game of soccer pitting the brothers against each other to Eleni. Andreas and Nikandros were hard-core fans of the game.

The simple idea spiraled into a national event.

Once she'd got both brothers to join, Mia soon found herself visiting the soccer clubs in the city, looking for players. She'd even called on a couple of her old colleagues. Soon, the two teams were filled with an assortment of players ranging from minor soccer celebrities to players from inner-city clubs.

That the Princes were playing a soccer game against each other became the social event of the summer. In over her head, but suddenly teeming with ideas, Mia had enlisted Eleni's help. Now the event was sold out at exorbitant prices and Mia's unofficial career was launched.

"This could be your thing, you know, your *platform* so to speak. Every princess needs one," Eleni had chirped, supreme satisfaction in her face.

"What's yours?"

She'd shrugged. And for the hundredth time, Mia had wondered if Eleni truly didn't mind her limbo status, being thought less than her brothers by the conventionalists in Drakon. For all her tireless endeavors, there was a steel wall around the Drakos sister. She butted into everyone's affairs and yet was fiercely private when it came to her own life. "I'm not officially a princess, Mia. More of a wizard behind the curtains type."

Mia had burst out laughing.

"Princess Mia, Patroness of Sports Charities," she'd said with relish. "It's something that fits your background, your image and it has a nice ring for the future wife of the Daredevil Prince. If I was the romantic sort, I would say Nik and you were made for each other."

Mia's gut bottomed out at Eleni's statement.

Nik and she, made for each other? Dare she believe it?

"Why do you look so shocked," Eleni had said, holding up two different jerseys she'd had designed for the two teams.

A dragon spewing fire with a soccer ball, or *football* as everyone seemed to correct her a thousand times a day, under its monstrous jaw was the common emblem on the teams' apparel.

Mia had rolled her eyes and bit into her lip, hard, to stop from laughing when Eleni had unveiled the logo for the first time at dinner with the aplomb of a queen— really, Drakonites and their obsession with dragons was hilarious.

She'd seen the same glimmer of humor in Nik's twinkling eyes and twitching mouth, but Eleni would skewer them if they so much as made a peep. Andreas, as usual, had just stared at the logo unblinkingly for a while, then returned his attention to his dinner.

"Once you marry and the baby comes, you're going to have your hands full. That is, if you and Nik are able to set aside this fierce competitive thing you've got going on.

"Did you know that there's a pool among the palace staff about whether you and Nik will come through this whole…opposing team debacle? Of all things, I can't believe people are getting this worked up over football." Apparently, it was informal but widespread knowledge that Nik and Mia were *together*.

Mia had somehow been roped into coaching Andreas's team as they were supposed to be the underdogs, against Nik's team which was full of athletes.

To Mia's everlasting shock, Nikandros seemed to have taken this as a personal insult. "If that's accusation I hear in your voice because I'm coaching Andreas and—"

"It just seems like a trick to provoke Nikandros—coaching the opposition's team. There's such a thing called masculine ego, Mia."

"Damn it, you're being just as irrational as Nik now. It's not as if I chose Andreas over him, Eleni."

"You know how competitive Nik can get."

Even dinners with the four of them had become a riot, Nik and Eleni ganging up against Mia and Andreas. With whom she'd been forced to form a reluctant alliance.

She still didn't trust the Crown Prince but she didn't think he was the diabolical control freak she'd thought him the first day.

When Nik's team was on the field at the same time as theirs for practice, she followed him across it greedily

taking in every word he said, every motion of that
sleekly honed body, every gesture, every smile.

Andreas had to wave his hands in front of her once to
get her attention. Even the mortification and the knowing smiles that she'd been caught gawking at Nik like
one of those royal groupies that seemed to follow him
around—one had even sneaked into the his private office once from the visitor tour—didn't stop her.

It morphed into this desperate ache inside her to be
by his side, to share that intimacy with him again.

With the amount of media exposure the game was
getting, her stupid moniker began to be bandied about
by the press again—Soccer Widow In Action Again
in Drakon, Soccer Widow's Ties to the Royal Family.

It felt really good to be doing something that she
loved, so Mia ignored the nonsensical headlines. But
she'd cursed the game as much as she enjoyed it, for
suddenly it seemed to create a chasm between Nik and
her again.

The day of the soccer match dawned sunny and crisp,
a perfect Drakonite summer day, filling the stadium
with people. Little Drakon flags abounded everywhere
Mia looked, a festive atmosphere permeating the palace and staff alike.

Dressed in shorts and a loose Team T that hid her
small belly, Mia went to the stadium with Eleni in a
tinted limo surrounded by a fleet of security vehicles.

The game turned out to be the most talked-about social event of the season. The entire nation tuned in to

watch their beloved Princes going head-to-head against each other.

Pregnancy hormones or not, even Mia had to fan herself quite a few times at the sight of those broad chests and muscular calves. She would never play again, but God, if it wasn't thrilling even to be on the sidelines.

Nikandros's team won in the end, but Andreas had been a revelation. He'd been feral on the field, as if something had come undone inside of him.

Nik's jersey had come off by the end of the game, to a loud applause from the crowd. That lean, rippling chest, the defined slab of muscle narrowing around his low-slung shorts—every woman had her eyes on him.

And of course, the charmer performed for them, waving, blowing kisses and throwing that megawatt smile.

The urge to march into the middle of that small field and plant her mouth on his chest, declare that he belonged to her, was so wild, so overwhelming that Mia had to empty out a chilled bottle of water over her head to cool down.

And Nik had seen that. While she stood there with water rippling down her face and neck, her emotions twisted and toppling, his eyes collided with hers, a dare in them.

Seeing a couple of reporters notice her, Mia forced herself to walk away from the field, even as every inch of her wanted to stay there and stake her claim. Back in their suite, she quickly showered and dressed in a light pink collared dress that boasted a straight, stiff bodice but touched her knees in a feminine frill.

Blow-drying her hair, she looked at her reflection and stared. The dress, casually chic and elegant, fit her to perfection. She was twelve weeks along but maybe because she'd been always slim and athletic in build, she wasn't quite showing yet.

Now that the game was over, the palace staff was in an uproar getting everything ready for tonight's celebration.

Drakonites and the world had already seen the brothers on the field in a friendly game. Tonight would be a welcome home party for Nikandros, a statement to the world that the Princes of Drakos would work for the progress of Drakon—a powerful statement unlike any the palace had made in the last two decades, according to Eleni.

The door swung open behind her and Nikandros walked in.

Thankfully, his jersey was back on. The lines of his face gleamed with satisfaction, the thrill of a good game won. His dark hair was slicked back with wetness and she realized he'd showered and changed like her. Vitality poured off his sun-kissed skin.

When he closed the heavy door behind him, the corded muscles in his arms had Mia swallowing the desire that seemed to uncurl in every inch of her.

With a slow gait, he strolled in and leaned against the arched wall, cutting off her way to the exit. Then set that blue gaze on her.

It traveled over her with such lingering leisure that all the pulse points in her body seemed to pound into life. Tension weaved thick in the air, winding around them.

"That dress…is it new?'

Breath ballooning in her chest, Mia stared unblinkingly. "Yes, do you like it?" He raised a brow and she babbled on. "It's from my new wardrobe," she finally managed, swallowing that teengaer-esque squeal that rose in her throat.

"You didn't congratulate me, Mia," he said in a careless drawl.

Mia smoothed the dress over her hips. All she'd wanted these past weeks was that he look at her, speak to her, and now that he was, all she could do was panic. Until that moment, she'd never realized what a tremendous coward she was.

She shrugged. "You didn't look like you'd miss it you were so busy performing for the crowd. I'm not a huge fan of pushing my way through throngs of your adoring female fans just to get to you." Even though it was exactly what she'd been dying to do. "Eleni's always lecturing me how I'm supposed to act all poised and disapproving of everyone and everything." She was exaggerating, but by God, she loved the crease he got in his cheek while he tried to intimidate her.

Because that's what this whole routine was.

But there was such a raw honesty about Nikandros, an edge of freedom to his emotions that it lured her in.

"Still, you're the opposing team's coach and it is good sportsmanship to congratulate the winning captain, *ne*?"

"Fine, congratulations," she said, slowly melting inside at his possessive look. "One would think I purposefully made the whole palace speculate that—"

He pushed off from the wall with a sinuous grace. Words got lost between her brain and her lips. He circled the room, touching all the small things she'd spread out around their suite, his gaze never leaving her. "One would not be wrong in assuming that you did it only to rile me seeing how chummy Andreas and you were being."

She colored. "That's ridiculous, Nik. You're taking this whole thing to extremes."

He had reached her now, and the scent of him—sweat and sun and skin—her throat filled up with him, the urge to rub herself against him a wild tattoo under her skin.

"I see," he said, a knot between his brows. It felt like she was waiting for a predator to strike. "So, Eleni is talking about how this should be an annual event. A soccer game between the Princes and a celebration in the evening."

Her mouth dry, Mia licked her lips. "That sounds like a good idea. A grand tradition, actually."

"So you would tell me that say, next year, I can form a team with all my exes and daughters from the highest echelons of Drakonite society and you wouldn't mind one jot?"

Hands bunched in his shirt, she tugged at him. "I'll mind that very much. I can't stand the thought of you with other women. I couldn't even bear to see those—" she moved her hand in the general direction of the field "—women looking at you. So, no, that would not be okay."

A fierce glitter filled his eyes then and his mouth lost that tight curve. "And?"

"Next time, I'll be on your team. Even though you're obviously the better athlete and Andreas needs—"

"Andreas is going to be the bloody King, *agapita*. He can find his own damn coach, for all I care."

She nodded like a good girl. "I'll only cheer your manly prowess and stare only at your extremely well-formed calves and other…parts of your anatomy."

Color rode high on his cheeks, his mouth twitching. "Ahhh…so you have a weakness for muscled calves and what other parts?"

"Tight asses," she said, tongue in cheek.

Brows lifted, mouth held tight, he stared at her with wide eyes. Nothing had ever felt so satisfactory as shocking Nikandros. Or as exciting.

His hands clutched her arms, and a growl vibrated from his chest. "Mine better be the only tight ass you were staring at, Mia."

Nikandros knew he was reacting like a petulant teenager about the friendship he'd seen emerge between Andreas and Mia. It had come to him one evening during dinner when they had all argued about a historical soccer game—how similar they were in temperament. Both played their cards very close to their hearts, and both had seen something in the other to allow them to let that guard down.

Though Nikandros had his own estate in the city, they would all be working in close quarters for years to come. That there was a tenuous bond between his future wife and his ruthless brother was a good thing, he'd reminded himself a million times.

And yet the way Andreas gained her confidence, the way Mia saw the cracks beneath that imperturbable facade of his, something even Eleni had missed—it made jealousy burn in Nik's chest.

Damn it, he'd spent so much of his life being second best to his brother. It didn't matter that Andreas himself had never treated him as such. It didn't matter that Nikandros had made a name for himself.

The irrational feeling that he was competing again, was in the same race, resenting Andreas for no fault of his… This whole situation with Mia was slowly driving him crazy.

Heat from her body made that subtle scent of roses that she preferred rise up toward him. *Christos*, he was going to implode from his desire for her.

Her fingers rested on his abdomen, and his muscles instantly clenched. The pink of her dress brought out all the warm tones of her honeyed skin. She looked like a voluptuous rose, her skin dewy smooth and petal soft. Her brown eyes shone; her face had lost that wraith-like look she'd worn the last year.

Being in Drakon suited Mia. She was forever hiding in the library or on her knees in the garden patch she'd asked for, her gaze following him around when she saw him with a mixture of concern and that artless desire.

And having Mia around, even when they were playing cat and mouse, he realized, suited him. Even when she and Andreas had been talking strategy, her presence had been a lodestone.

Her throat moved.

He followed the elegant line of it, to the delicate crook of her neck to her breasts, to the indent of her waist that the dress neatly delineated. He ran a finger tracing the curve of it and inhaled deep. "I haven't asked how you've been feeling of late."

"Hungry. Sometimes hormonal. But good. I found an ob-gyn that I like."

"Good." And then he asked what he'd been dying to do for days.

"Can I touch you?"

She nodded, eyes wide in her face. Slowly, he laid his palm flat on her stomach and frowned. "You feel the same." He moved his palm to the sides, and only then felt the subtle convexity of her stomach.

Breath punched into his throat.

He could feel even that small change because she'd had such a flat, toned abdomen. A band of tight muscles that he'd licked on his way to other inviting places.

She put her hand on his and held it there, a glow like he'd never seen in her face. "Some women just show it slowly—that's what the ob-gyn said."

He nodded. It sank in now, what they'd created together. Only now, he realized how momentous this was. So many things could go wrong but, *Thee Mou*, he wanted to do this right. He wanted to be a good husband, a good father, he wanted to treasure what Mia had brought into his life.

He would do this right.

CHAPTER TEN

MIA WRAPPED HER arms around Nikandros, hoping he would hold her. She so desperately longed to feel his strength around her, longed to banish whatever demons drove him to work at that breakneck pace.

Between ordering a new wardrobe, figuring out a new regimen for exercise and finding a new gynecologist in the city, the more she learned of Nik, the more Mia realized what a complex man he was.

That she had compared him to Brian, she was realizing, was an insult to the man who was so much more than he'd ever been.

And Mia with each passing day was being twined into his life. The worst was, she'd begun to care less and less about it, a future away from Drakon and Nik becoming more and more vague.

The shudder that went through him as his hand stayed on her tummy was slight but she knew exactly how he felt. How inconsequential everything else felt when they considered the tiny life they'd made together.

He pulled back from her just as abruptly as he'd held

her. Ran a hand over his forehead and then his neck, and turned away.

"You were right. You should move to another suite. I'm working a lot of late nights to sign this deal with this new investor Gabriel Marquez and I will only disturb your sleep.

"Eleni has told me that you're tiring soon these days."

Her throat tight, Mia tried to understand her own feelings. She felt like the flower she'd spent months tending to had suddenly died on her.

The sense of loss was so acute that she automatically ran a hand over her tummy.

She stared around the suite with the lovely drapes and the massive king bed. The veranda that offered a gorgeous view of the spectacularly maintained gardens. The suite had become more home to her than the apartment she'd shared with a colleague or even the beachfront property Brian had insisted they needed.

But it wouldn't be home without Nikandros.

She hadn't known one since she had walked away from her parents. But this was her home, wherever Nikandros was.

Nothing in her life was going to be the same without him in it. But for once, the fear that came with that realization was submerged by how strongly she wanted to be with him. To experience the intimacy of that night again.

There had been an openness between them that night, an urgency because they thought they would never see each other again.

She wanted that Nik again. She wanted to be that Mia again.

She wanted all their nights to be like that night. And she was damned if she didn't at least fight for it.

"You're the one who insisted that we should work on our relationship."

"I'll still be in the palace, Mia. I'll have the staff coming and going all the time. It's better if you—"

"You work like a demon. With the soccer game over, we don't even have practice and I'll hardly ever see you."

"We'll still have dinner every night."

That helplessness slowly morphed into anger. Why was he pushing her away, just when she was beginning to see what she wanted? Just when she was learning to reach for it? "Andreas and Eleni will be there. That's not the same as—" She moved to block him, copying his own move earlier. "I don't want to sleep alone. I've gotten used to waiting on the chaise for you."

A fire smoldered in his eyes then. And for the first time in her life, Mia understood what was going on. He was wound up as tight as she was. Then why was he bent on putting distance between them?

"It's not good for your back. Just sleep on the damn bed. I'll come and check on you every night."

"But—"

"*Thee mou*, Mia, don't make this hard."

Her temper splintered like the crack of thunder. "I'm making this hard? Damn it, Nik!

"You pretty much kidnap me from Miami. You insist that we do the right thing by our child. You damn near make it impossible for me to resist you.

"And now, now…when I can't go through a single hour in the day without thinking of you, when I'm damn near combusting because I want to kiss you and touch you so badly…now…you want to keep your distance?"

"Mia…"

"No, you listen to me!" She was shouting now, like she'd never done. Her throat was raw with unshed tears, her heart so achingly full.

She'd never needed anyone in her life as she did Nikandros, with this quiet desperation.

"I don't want to sleep alone. I don't want the little time we spend with each other diluted by Andreas's and Eleni's presence. And I sure as hell don't want you to shut me out in the guise of work and your bloody deal.

"Which, by the way, has completely consumed you so much that you have dark circles under your eyes and you walk around like a grumpy bear chewing the head off anyone who dares to speak to you.

"I want you with me here." She bent her head to his chest, a twisting ache moving through her. "Please, Nik." Her hands moved up the rigid line of his spine to the tight clench in his shoulders, up his nape, and sank into his hair.

He felt so good in her hands, so wonderfully solid and male around her. She never wanted to leave his embrace. Even with the fear that he would crush her heart, Mia still wanted to run toward him.

Scrunching his hair around her fingers, she tugged until he was bent toward her, until she could look into those blue eyes that had begun to mean the world to her. Pressing her mouth to his jaw, she breathed him in. Found the furor in her gut calming. When had he become her anchor?

"Won't you make love to me again, *carino*? I need you quite desperately. I feel as if I'll unravel if you won't kiss me, Nikandros."

A tight vein pounded in his temple as he tugged her face up. His fingers twisted her hair with something close to pain, his breath pulsing like wildfire against her skin. A conflagration began in Mia's body, setting every nerve ending on fire. "If we do this, there's no going back, Mia."

His hot mouth moved over her jaw, down to her neck. The drag of his teeth over the pulse in her neck.

A rush of wetness pooled between her thighs. Instinctively she clenched them to hold that ache there but he shoved a muscled thigh between hers.

With the rub of her tender folds against his thigh, a sob burst out of her throat.

"No, *glykia mou*. That shiver between your thighs is mine. Your arousal, every little quiver of your body, every inch of you will be mine from now on, Mia.

"No more time to be had before you get used to the idea of marriage.

"No more second thoughts.

"No more running scared.

"For the rest of your life, you'll be the Daredevil Prince's wife and the mother of his children."

The stark possessiveness of his statements twisted through the deepest recesses of her heart, smashing through any armor she'd left against him. Instead of terrifying her, his words sent an illicit thrill through her. She nodded, the idea of never withholding anything from this man forever releasing her from her own fears.

"Children, you said children," she whispered against his neck as he carried her to the bed. She licked the strong pulse there and tasted salt and soap and skin.

The taste of him exploded on her tongue and she did it again.

Felt his chest rumble at her side when she dug her teeth into a tight shoulder.

With nimble fingers, he pulled her dress off and stripped his own clothes.

Sunlight kissing the hard planes of his body, he was a sight to behold. Fingers gripping her ankles, he pushed her onto the bed and climbed over her. "You didn't think we were going to stop with this one, did you?"

Mia barely comprehended that he was answering her question with one of his own as his palm splayed on her tummy before moving onto the seam of her panties and pulling them down.

"We're not?" she somehow managed amidst the drum of her heart in her ears.

"No, we're not," came his gruff answer.

His torso twisting sideways, he threw the wadded ball of the silky fabric, giving her a glimpse of a tight butt cheek. She'd been so intent on what he revealed of her that night that she hadn't feasted on the masculine splendor that was his body.

Flesh stretched tight over his chest that tapered to

lean hips. His thighs—Mia swallowed, remembering the corded strength of those long muscles when he'd pushed into her the last time. Like her own body, his had been honed, and that contained power of his sent a thrum through her.

He turned around. His shaft was long and thick, protruding out.

Heat rose through Mia, tingling from head to toe, merging into an ache at her sex. With her elbows, she pushed herself up and wrapped her fingers around him.

Such hardness encased in such velvet silk—he was beautiful. She fisted her hands and pumped up and down. The veins in his neck stood out in stark relief before his fingers clamped over her wrist.

"Not today, Mia. No playing today. No slow loving, *agapi mou*. I need you too much and I'm going to take you hard and fast." Even his deep rasp couldn't hide the question.

"You inside me, Nik, that's all I care about."

"Good."

And then he pushed her back onto the bed, his hands roving over her restlessly.

"We're going to make our own football team and you, Mia Rodriguez Morgan, are going to be the coach."

"Don't I have a say in whether I want a brood of little daredevils to run after the rest of my life?"

His fingers stilling on the straps of her bra, he looked into her eyes and burst into laughter.

God, she could spend all eternity like this, listening to the sound of his laughter. An eternity soaking in the warmth of that smile. "Little daredevils? You've only yourself to blame for putting that image in my head, *pethi mou*.

"Now I'm even more determined."

Her bra came off, his rough fingers pinching the taut nipples.

Back arching off the bed, Mia pushed into his touch. Eyes glittering, he bent his head and licked one dark bud. That sculpted mouth pressed wet kisses around it. "I'm sure I can persuade you of the merits of the idea," he whispered, and then closed his mouth over her nipple. The relentless flicks of his tongue sent pulses of sensation pounding to her core.

And made that rhythmic motion with his mouth rend her in two with blinding pleasure.

Panting and sobbing, Mia tried to move her lower body. He didn't let her.

He tugged and sucked and licked and stroked until she thought she would die from the pleasure of it. Whorls of pleasure eddied in her lower belly and she pressed her wet sex wantonly against one hair-dusted thigh.

A trail of hot kisses between the valley of her breasts followed. Fingers twisting in the sheets, her pelvis rocking against him, Mia was mindless with need.

With his hands on her knees, he widened her.

Mia stiffened.

"All of you… Mia."

Desire pinching his features, he pushed until she relented. Her thighs fell away as his fingers tested her dampness. Her flesh closed over his fingers eagerly when he penetrated her, like a flower furling its petals tight.

"You're so perfect. So damn tight."

With a raw groan, Mia held on to his shoulders as he settled heavily between her legs. His long fingers gripping her thighs roughly, he lifted her pelvis and entered her in a deep thrust.

Stars exploded at the back of Mia's eyes. He was hot and hard inside her, sending swirls of ache. He tilted her and went deeper, filling her with that thickness.

Mia screamed at the tight friction and came in a violent burst of pleasure. And still, there was a knot in her chest, a tight pit of fear that made her shudder all over.

The pleasure and the intimacy—it made fear bubble up inside her.

A mixture of panic and something else flared deep in her as he began to pull out. She curled her fingers around his arms, desperate to never lose him just as her pelvic muscles clenched tight around him.

"Slow down, Mia. Open your eyes, and look at me."

"You're going to be end of me."

Her eyes remained tight shut. She'd never felt so raw and vulnerable. Every part of her heart stood naked in his arms.

If she opened her eyes, he would know. He would see how deeply she had fallen in love with him. He would know how much the thought terrified her. She tilted her head to the side, fighting against the tears seeping hot against her eyelids.

"Will you not look at me, Mia? Will you not share this with me completely?"

Her eyes flew open. "I'm here, Nik. All of me." Her

throat rasped to get the words out. With a shaking hand, she traced the proud lines of his face, cradled him in her palm. Her heart felt like it would never stop expanding in her chest. "More than I've ever been present in any moment in my life. And this…how good it feels, the magic of this moment…it terrifies me, Nik.

"If anything happens to this…whatever it is we share, I couldn't bear it. I would shatter completely."

"But nothing will happen to this, Mia. I won't let it," he said, peppering soft, slow kisses against her temple.

And then he began to move inside her again.

Deep and fast, with a visceral need that destroyed her and remade her.

He took her with no reprieve, with no false gentleness. He pounded into her welcoming flesh, as if he too, like her, was trying to still the moment here.

Fingers digging into his buttocks, Mia tilted her pelvis the next time to meet his thrust.

"Yes, just like that, Mia *mou*. Move with me. Trust your body."

Soft need spread its fingers through her swollen muscles again as she moved in concert with his body, learning his rhythm, learning to trust that primal desire she'd always repressed with a tight fist.

The friction was intense, bone-melting and when he pulled her closer and swirled his hips with an erotic mastery, Mia went flying again.

Her name a mantra on his lips, Nikandros followed her with one last thrust, and then collapsed on top of her with a shudder that racked his entire frame.

A damp sheen coated his skin. Slowly returning to

the world around her, Mia pressed her forehead to his shoulder and breathed in the scent that they made.

Every emotion she'd ever felt—pain, anger, fear—everything seemed to fade into colorlessness at the love that filled her.

It was a raging pulse in her throat, an ache in her chest, a helplessness in her gut. And a smile that blossomed on her mouth when he moved to his side, gathered Mia tight in his arms and said, "Team Nikandros, then."

Nikandros was standing at the ramparts one evening looking out at Drakon and the harbor beyond. All of Gabriel's demands had been met. He was arriving in a few days and new ground would be broken for the construction of a resort in less than a week.

The thrill of the chase filled him. In ten years, the face of Drakon would change completely and it would be his name on it.

Not Andreas Drakos.

Not Theos Drakos.

But him.

His little legacy in the annals of history—the runt's legacy.

Nikandros turned around when he sensed Mia close by.

"Was it a good day at the office, honey?" she called out, tilting her head to the side.

That irreverent wit of hers made him smile. "Come here."

When she was close enough, he wrapped his arms around her and sighed.

"This used to be my favorite haunt as a child. I'd tell myself I was a knight and would save the castle from enemies.

"I couldn't wait to join my father and brother and make them proud of me. Make Drakon proud of me."

"Why him, Nik?" Now, weeks later, when she saw precious little of Nikandros, Mia understood Andreas's misgivings. Appointments and meetings, everything that wasn't related to Drakon was pushed back by Nik's aides, claiming that the Prince didn't have time. "Don't tell me he's the only investor you could find for Drakon."

"Why not Gabriel? That deal fell through years ago because of what I did. It's my mess to clean up now. It was another of my failures as far as Theos was concerned."

She looked up at him, fear wedging in her throat. "Does it matter if you succeed here, Nik? You've made a name for yourself in the world. Anything you touched, you've made it into gold.

"Isn't that fierce need satisfied now? I know how passionate you are about Drakon. I just wish… I wish you'd slow down."

He shrugged, swallowing away his shock. So many things about Mia were a revelation. Her perception, the way she cared for everyone around her even as she carefully guarded herself.

There was something so artless, so real about her that every other relationship he'd ever had, every possession, every success seemed to fade when he looked at Mia.

"I wish I could, Mia. But something happens to me between these walls."

Exhaling roughly, he looked down at her just as she clasped his unshaven cheek. She was so fragile and fine boned in his hands, and yet the pulse under her fingers pounded in a frantic rhythm.

Soon, she was going to swell with his baby, and here he was, still dwelling on the demons in his past. Still letting its poisonous shadow mar his present.

But there was no future without facing the past, and he'd been driving himself at an insane pace. He'd never been a man who did anything in half measures, never been afraid to leap into the unknown with nothing but a rope in the dark. Right or wrong, weak or strong, he'd lived life by his own rules.

And it meant showing Theos what he was capable of, before his father fell down that final slide into madness.

"Is this more important than what we build, Nik? Does this deal…does success in Drakon matter beyond what it means to us as a family?"

"It is a fresh start, Mia. For you and me, in a Drakon in which I have earned my place."

Hadn't he already done that a thousand times over?

Suddenly, Mia realized why he was doing this. Why he had been killing himself, working around the clock chasing Gabriel Marquez, ensuring that every demand of his was met.

He wanted to close this deal before his father was gone. This was, in his mind, the last chance to show his father what he was made of.

Having dealt with Andreas, having heard of all the

ways King Theos had abused and played with his children, she was terrified of what he would say to Nikandros. She felt the most overpowering urge to steal him away from Drakon.

To not let the shadow of it mar their future.

A part of Nikandros's heart would always belong to his country. No one could change it—not Theos, not Andreas, not even Mia. Not all of them together.

It wasn't Isabella's hold over him that she had to worry about. It was Drakon's.

It was having to walk away from Drakon that had made Nikandros so hard and ruthless, that had only left mere traces of the generous man she glimpsed.

What little there was of his heart, it was occupied by Drakon.

The realization pressed against her chest.

But nothing she said could change his mind. And Mia was terrified that telling him even the biggest truth of her life wouldn't be enough. So she kept quiet, hoping for the best. Hoping that Nikandros, as always, would emerge the victor, and then, he would be free to accept her love. And maybe love her in return too.

As he held her within the circle of his arms, Mia closed her eyes and breathed the scent of him deep into her lungs.

In a million years, she wouldn't meet a man like Nik. A man who lived life to the fullest, a man who made every minute, every day brighter, a man who cared endlessly. Her heart felt full, bursting to the seams as he kissed her temple and pulled her with him.

He took her to bed and made love to her with a passion that was never ending. Through the days that came next, he laughed with her when they were in bed. He laid his head on her stomach and talked to the baby, even though she told him the baby couldn't know him yet.

In the darkest time before dawn, he talked of how the future would look once he and Mr. Marquez took on Drakon—how bright it was going to be, how everything was going to be all right.

As if happiness was still a vague concept that had to be achieved.

As if it wasn't in the here and now, in those wonderful moments he gave her when he'd arranged a greenhouse for her, and then christened it by making love to her there, when he'd stood by her when she'd called her mom to tell her that she was going to get married soon, when he'd screamed his pleasure the time that Mia had gone down on her knees and told him she wanted to make his darkest fantasy true.

As if he wasn't already the perfect man.

And Mia laughed and listened as if she wasn't already irrevocably in love with him.

Even as she tried, she knew that the thirst to prove himself to his father consumed him, worse than any addiction, worse than any high he could have chased.

If she lost him, she had no walls to defend herself against the oncoming storm, no way to remake herself, because Nikandros was life itself to her.

CHAPTER ELEVEN

"PLEASE, NIK. CAN'T you say your goodbyes from here?"

From the moment Mia had whispered the words against his chest as dawn streaked the sky, Nik knew something was going to go wrong.

His instincts had saved his life more than once. And today they said to leave the past alone where it was. But when had he done the conventional thing?

He had achieved everything he'd set out to do and he couldn't rest until he faced his father one more time. He couldn't look toward the future until he laid his struggles with his father to rest.

So he joined Andreas in the tinted limo.

The vehicle sped away from the palace, leading to the estate where his father had been "convalescing" for the last few years.

And slowly, as they left the city behind and drove the mountainous region dotted with small villages nestled in its foothills, Andreas said, "You will receive quite a shock when you see him, Nik. As will he.

"He becomes agitated quite easily and will not calm down soon." Hands fisted, knuckles white, Andreas laughed with a bitterness that sent chills down Nik's spine. "He did not go into convalescence easily, Nik. I forced him. He was destroying peace talks, he wanted to increase taxation, he was talking of marrying again… he was arranging an alliance with one of his cronies—a sixty-year-old man for Eleni.

"I had to stop him."

"I don't blame you for what you had to do, Andreas. For God's sake, you put up with him for long enough. If it's guilt talking…"

His brother however wasn't even listening. "So he went kicking and screaming, spewing vitriol at me, at my mother, at anyone he could think of. And then he told me of something he'd done all those years ago."

Nikandros had never seen his brother like that. So furious and fierce, as if the seams of his control were finally ripping apart. "Andreas?"

"When he sees you today, he's going to lose it. And I need him sane."

The limo came to a sudden stop and Nikandros never heard what his brother had been about to say.

Nursing staff was in an uproar around the white-washed building that was nestled against a small hill. The water from the streams added a continuous swish; the rock faces around the villa were sharp and craggy.

All Nik heard in the chaos was that his father had somehow broken out of his room.

Andreas was yelling for details when Nik saw him. Nikandros patted Andreas on the back to get his attention when he saw the lone figure atop a jagged rock.

Nikandros had never run so fast in his life. He and Andreas circled around to reach Theos from either side.

Silver abundantly threading through his hair, their father looked gaunt and so skinny that his flesh hung in folds over his face. But his eyes, those electric ice-blue eyes that Nik had inherited, were still sharp, looking out from sunken sockets.

"Nikandros?" he heard Theos say in a raspy voice as if he'd quite forgotten how to speak.

"Yes, Father. Take my hand and we will walk down."

Theos looked at Nik's hand as if it were a weapon. "Is it true that you brought Gabriel Marquez back into Drakon?"

Nik couldn't hide his shock. When he looked at Andreas, all he could see was a cold fire of hatred. "I still have my spies, Nikandros. Your brother has done every cruel thing to threaten me but there are still those who are loyal to me. Who'll protect my secrets even after I'm gone."

A curse ripped from Andreas and Theos flinched.

"Andreas and I are going to rebuild Drakon with Gabriel's investment," Nik said, only to pull Theos's attention back to him.

There was a murderous rage in his brother's eyes that sent a ripple of alarm down his spine. All he felt was pity for Theos but it was Andreas Nik wanted to protect in that moment. Andreas whose cold fury seemed bone deep.

"So I did make a good bet on you then." Vicious satisfaction settled onto his father's bones.

Nik said, "What do you mean?" the same moment Andreas said, "Leave it alone, Nik."

"I married your mother because the DNA test proved that you were a boy. Camille was nothing but a royal groupie who gave herself to me. No better than the nanny that had Eleni. She was of common blood. But I needed another heir.

"Except the doctors told me you were of no use to me from the moment you were born.

"In the end, my genes did win out. You have made me proud, Nikandros. You have earned your place in the House of Drakos."

Barely had his father's words registered in his brain when Andreas reached him. "Come away from the edge, Father. We have unfinished business."

Theos sent a pleading glance toward Nik. "I still can declare you the Crown Prince, Nik. All I ask is you keep your brother away from me."

Andreas did no more than growl, but his father panicked, backed away. And then slipped on one of the mossy rocks. Before either of his sons could reach him, King Theos fell to his death with a sob and a scream, a manic glitter in his eyes.

Hours later, Nikandros stood in his brother's office, waiting for Andreas, the specter of his father's death still looming large in his mind. He rubbed a shaking hand over his face, the truth of this afternoon a huge boulder on his chest.

Of course, everything made sense now. His mother and father had never quite stayed together, even married, and she'd left as soon as she'd known Nik was well. He could just imagine Theos taunting her for her supposed cheating of him, and giving him a runt.

All these years, Nik knew, she'd only sought to protect him from the bitter truth. Andreas was right. His ill health had been his salvation.

And yet that nagging ache persisted. He'd stayed at the estate the rest of the day, arranging people to transport his father's body to the state hospital. There would be an autopsy, a statement from the doctors. While Eleni and Andreas worked with their PR teams to come up with a statement to release to the people.

Theos had been bitter, poisonous to the end, still pitting his sons against each other. That he could still mourn that man shocked him.

"Did you get the answer you came for?" Andreas said, walking into the room.

"Yes. I wanted him to know what I had achieved for Drakon. And I wanted to know why he had always been so cruel to me."

"You had a mother who adored you. And now you have more with Mia. You have escaped the same fate as me."

Theos had cost him his brother—a brother he'd only learned recently was far from the cold bastard Nik had called him on so many occasions.

Hands shoved in the pockets of his trousers, Andreas said, "I'll be leaving immediately after the funeral. I need time away from the palace."

"What about Drakon?"

"I wish he had been alive longer if only to see Drakon's economy shine like a jewel under your leadership. Drakon has you."

Nikandros had barely whispered yes and his brother walked away, leaving Nikandros with everything he had wanted once and yet nothing. Andreas had reduced his achievements into a neat little summary.

There were a million matters to attend to, and he gave them his attention.

But in the days that followed, he couldn't seem to shake off his father's words, nor the chill that came with them. When his mother came to the palace, he held her diminutive form tight against him, breathing in the scent of her.

He felt like that sick, young boy who had clung to her, wishing for his father's presence. He hadn't been enough; nothing he'd done would ever have been enough for Theos.

But to discover that he'd still loved his father, that his love and his need for Theos's approval had brought him to this grief, it was like a festering wound.

And Mia... He couldn't look her in the eye without betraying the emotion that flooded him every time she came near.

He couldn't stand her pity. She'd begged him not to see his father. But, she said nothing either, giving herself to him when he needed her.

A dizzy joy flooded him every time he smelled the rose scent of her; emotion clutched his throat.

He had the eerie feeling that he was following in Theos's footsteps. The only reason Mia and he were marrying was for the child. No, he would never be so calculatingly cruel like his father; he would never neglect his child so much. And still, was he not repeating history, just for a different reason?

Was he not tying himself to another person who had never wanted to be married in the first place? Would she have chosen him if not for the baby, if not for his insistence?

Would that taunt him for the rest of his life like Theos's lack of approval had, taint his relationship with Mia forever?

Because, after everything that had happened, contrary to his father's final words, Nikandros found out he was weak after all.

He would always crave what he was denied. He would always crave love of the deepest level, because that's what he did.

He loved fiercely. He didn't know any other way.

Maybe being shielded from the cruelties of the world for so many years had changed his makeup forever.

And he loved Mia with every breath in him.

And soon, he knew now, he would resent Mia for having that power over him, for not returning it the same way, for always being out of his reach forever.

Christos, he couldn't spend his life like that. He would ruin both their lives and their child's.

And as for Drakon crying for heirs, they could all go to hell.

Only an environment of love would offset the bloody sacrifices it demanded. The thought of sending her away almost was unbearable but he had to do it.

Andreas was leaving; Gabriel was waiting to begin.

In the days that followed, with Eleni on his side, he worked with the palace media team. His approval ratings went up when Gabriel and he released a statement heralding the new era in Drakon's history, the new image Drakon was going to achieve in the world's eyes as its number one luxury destination.

Critics that had before called him the Reckless Prince, a stain on the proud House of Drakon, now called him its salvation.

Nikandros, it seemed, finally had everything he had ever wanted and yet, in the blink of a day had lost everything too. For what he wanted most was love, and he'd realized too late that he couldn't force it.

Every fear that Mia had felt came true in the following weeks, starting with the news of King Theos's death.

Nikandros worked around the clock with Eleni and the palace staff, taking on more and more of the central duties expected of the Crown Prince, even more feverish and ruthless in driving the staff.

Mia had never felt so helpless. The more she tried to talk to Nik, the more he kept her at a distance. Distance between them seemed to grow even as they sat on either side of the table every night. All he'd tell her was that Drakon needed him right now.

What about me, she wanted to say but held back the selfish words.

But he was shutting her out, and she had no way to reach him.

The only time she felt close to him, the only time

she felt that he was there with her was when he made love to her.

For weeks following King Theos's death, Drakon went into mourning.

But the pall the King's death cast over his sons wouldn't let up.

From everything she'd heard of the hateful old man, it seemed like he was determined to ruin his son's lives even from beyond death.

The day of the funeral came and went.

The flowers in her garden were in full bloom, a riot of color and yet as one week merged into the next, Mia saw less and less of Nikandros.

He grew moody and distant. Whenever Mia tried to talk about King Theos or Andreas, he told her to leave it alone.

Andreas hadn't been seen again after the funeral. No one knew where he was, not even Eleni. And then she'd heard of Nik's overseas trip.

Unable to take any more tension, she went looking for Nik and found him in his office, standing at the window behind a huge mahogany desk.

"Nikandros?" she whispered, trying to quiet the alarm in her gut.

He turned. He looked tired, his smile worn. "You must have heard I'm leaving in a couple of hours."

"I would've liked to have heard it from you."

He raised a brow.

"That never intimidated me, and it doesn't awe me anymore," she snapped.

"I'll be gone for at least a month, if not more."

"That long?"

He didn't look the least bit worried about it. "Andreas had an upcoming tour to the Middle East that I would like to not miss. With him gone, there's a lot to do."

"Is he okay? Have you heard from him?"

"No, but I'm sure he's fine, Mia." Even as he dismissed her concern, she could see the worry in his eyes. Whatever the shadows of the past, Nik would never stop caring about his family. But did he care about her too?

Or had she already been relegated to the challenges he'd conquered?

"I know you've really been wanting to see your mother. You should go see her, take a break from the morbid atmosphere here in the palace." A sort of strained laugh fell from his mouth. Devoid of that energy of his, devoid of the pure joy he had found in life.

It was the most nauseating sound she'd ever heard in her life. Like he was only acting and playing his role, as if the spark was gone and a shell was left.

"You're asking me to go away? When you need me the most?"

"I do not need you, Mia. I do not need anything except peace to process everything that's been happening."

"And I'm somehow thwarting you from that?" she taunted, tears like needles in her throat.

"Last time, you needed time. This time it's me. With Andreas gone, everything's changed. My priorities are all Drakon now, and I just…

"I'll have no time for you. You should spend the time with your mom and sister. Maybe have the baby there.

"I'll come see you when I can."

He was lying. Nikandros, who had always given voice to the truth, even when it was hard, even when it was wrong, was lying.

"You're lying. You won't come to see me. You're sending me away and I don't even know what I did wrong." Her misery morphed into fury. "What did I do wrong, Nik?"

"*Christos*, Mia! There's no need to get so emotional about such a small matter. And this…this constant worry I see in your eyes, I don't need it.

"Drakon is enough of a stress point, and truly, it's not even the right time for us to marry."

It was the last thing Mia thought to hear from his mouth. She'd expected him to grieve for his father. She'd expected him to shut her out. She'd told herself to be patient, that he would find his way back to her again.

But this… She didn't know what to think anymore.

Had it become too much for him already? Was he bristling at the shackles their relationship put on him?

"You don't want to marry me anymore?" Unbidden tears rose and she locked them away. "Whatever happened to honesty, Nik?"

Taut lines spread from his mouth as he reached her. "You're right. Everything has changed. I have changed from the man who demanded that we marry for the sake of a child.

"Marriage for me now is not an emotional, impulsive move but a political one. It cannot be about one child and one woman.

"For now, I can't marry.

"And without both of us being a hundred percent

sure of it, marriage will only be a battleground for resentment. Neither of us wants that."

Mia didn't reply. She didn't think she could if she even tried.

Knees shaking, she closed the door behind him and walked away.

If her heart was breaking, she didn't even know. For she was chilled through and through like never before.

"Why did you send her away?"

Nikandros turned around in the balcony.

His sister was glaring at him.

It had been two weeks since Mia had left. He hoped she'd seen her mother and sister, hoped she was in the bosom of her family. He hoped they understood how much Mia loved them, how it had hurt her all these years to cut herself away from them.

"Because I'm a coward. And because I love her."

Eleni snorted, even though concern filled her eyes. "I didn't think you were the martyr type, Nik."

"No. I've finally learned self-preservation, sister of mine. I've learned the price of living recklessly, without control. I've learned that my heart can't bear any more scars.

"And with the mad King gone and our dear brother disappearing to God knows where, I have to protect myself, *ne*? At least, until Andreas returns."

Eleni stared at him, shock painting the tired angles of her face. "I never thought you would be like the rest of your stupid, imbecilic sex, brother of mine."

"Hey!" Nikandros swatted her halfheartedly. It was

impossible to keep up the cheerful, everything-is-fine facade with his sister. God, he was bone-tired and he had miles to go before the week was over.

The endless, cheerless, *thankless* tasks that his brother had kept up with all these years without a complaint edged in sidewise, Nikandros was in awe of him. And this was without Theos criticizing or second-guessing or dissecting every decision.

He had resented Andreas for his closeness with their father for so long—this had to be fate's punishment for him.

Eleni joined him at the railing. For so long, she'd been his brother's rock. And now she was his. "What do you mean?"

"How does loving Mia make you weak, Nik? You thrive on emotion. You live your life by sheer instinct. You said there was nothing more freeing and more challenging than taking whatever life threw at you."

"Yes, but it also makes me want everything, Eleni. I love her more than life itself and I can't live with anything less.

"I hope our brother returns before I'm forever shackled to this palace though. The idea of Drakon without Andreas is ridiculous."

"But you're here."

"I'm not him."

"No, you're not. You're you. You're the heart among the three of us, Nik. Father was truly mad for not seeing what he had. Andreas is Drakon's pride, but you... you're its heart, Nikandros. The spirit of those first warriors, it's in you.

"You're passion, you're laughter. You're life itself."

"And what are you, Ellie?"

"Adhesive."

Nikandros burst out laughing. He rubbed his eyes. Worry for Andreas was gnawing at his gut. "He needs us to hold the fort for him. I believe he will return. Tell the press that he's gone on an expedition to the North Pole."

"What?"

"That's what he said he wanted to do."

"You think he went there?"

"No. But wherever he went, he will return soon."

Eleni stayed silent, leaning into him. Nikandros draped his arm around her, wondering how a person could leave a hole in one's life.

"Ask her to come back, Nik. Persuade her that you've come to your senses again. Tell her it's the right thing for the child."

"No. It's her choice now, Ellie. I can't spend the rest of my life wondering if she'll love me. Wondering if she stayed with me because it was the safe choice, the sane choice."

"Sane, Nik? No woman who's sane will choose the roller coaster that your life is. She loves you, Nikandros, Can't you see that?"

"If she does, she will return. And if not, I'll have to let her go."

Eleni sighed. "Gabriel Marquez is your dining guest tonight."

A groan fell out of Nik's mouth. *Christos*, he was tired like he'd never been before. For more than a fortnight, he'd been running around.

And with Mia gone, the suite was like a crypt. After the first night, he'd even given up trying to sleep.

Now he was the one who swam at midnight, tiring himself out so that sleep came like oblivion.

The last thing he wanted was to deal with Gabriel.

"I can keep him company tonight, if you'd like. Stall him with some excuse. I can have my pick of them with Father's death and Andreas's disappearance. He'll understand, Nik."

"I can't fob him off on you, any more than I can let you work around the clock as you've been doing, Ellie. What about the holiday you planned to go on? What about the plans for your own life?" Their sister had always been just there. With a kind word and smile for him, with no-nonsense advice for Andreas, neatly arranging everything in their life without receiving even a thank-you in return.

Was there anyone Andreas and he had done right by? Was this the legacy Theos had left them? Was this why Andreas had needed to escape?

The questions and the ache they left in him were relentless.

His sister shied away from him and shrugged. "Really, Nik, one night of playing hostess to Mr. Marquez is not going to kill me.

"And I'm not leaving everything on your shoulders. With Andreas gone, you're going to be drowning as it is.

"As to my future, Drakon is it."

Something in her tone snagged at Nik, but he couldn't for the life of him pinpoint it.

He fell back into the bed again, and instantly, the

scent of roses filled his head. The knot in his gut clenched tight, a pulse of pain twisting deep inside him.

Thee mou, he missed her so much.

He missed her anxiety for him. He missed the warm cocoon her body had offered after a tired night. He missed the color passion painted her dusky skin.

It was as if there was a gaping hole in his gut.

But if he'd let her stay, he'd have resented her, and his love for her.

And he couldn't bear the poison that would have spewed in both their lives.

CHAPTER TWELVE

ARRANGING TO ARRIVE at the King's Palace, with her mother and Emmanuela in tow, without Nikandros knowing about it turned out be a logistical nightmare that wouldn't have been possible without Eleni's help.

But after so many years, Mia didn't want to leave her mother behind. Without Mia saying it out loud, her mother had understood how terrified Mia was.

For all she knew, she'd made a wasted trip across the Atlantic only to face more rejection. But Mia couldn't give up without a fight.

Nikandros needed her, whether he admitted it or not. She'd seen how grief for his father had ravaged him; she'd seen how Andreas's leaving had torn him apart. Instead of taking him in hand, she'd let him push her away. Believed in his false words when from the beginning, he had shown her with his actions what she meant to him.

If what it took was to wear him down, then she would.

When she'd asked after Andreas because she wanted to borrow a bit of his dry unflappability, Eleni had told her he still wasn't back.

It was more than a month and Nikandros, she said,

was sinking under the new investment ventures with Gabriel and the regular duties he was carrying on be-half of the palace.

Which made Mia's throat clench and she became even more determined that he needed her by his side. Now it was her turn.

She didn't know big, flowery words, but she wanted to surprise him, show him how much he meant to her. And if she had to spend the rest of her life proving that she adored him, she would.

She'd demanded, not requested, shamelessly that Eleni find her the best hair stylist and makeup artist she could command in one afternoon. And a ball gown that no other woman would wear tonight. And jewelry fit for the woman that would stand on the arm of the Daredevil Prince.

Shock plastered over her gamine features, Eleni said drily, "Do you want a diamond-studded tiara too?"

"If it could be managed, yes," Mia had replied with-out a beat. "And, Eleni, can you stay with me too?"

Eleni had thrown her head back and let out a loud whoop, and said thank God, Mia was finally growing into the role of being Princess of Drakon.

And in a mere couple of hours, everything had been arranged.

Mia and Eleni had spent the afternoon sipping Daiquiris—virgin for Mia—and being shown a parade of ball gowns ranging from frothy to severe, from silk so soft to necklines so low that she'd bare her navel.

And then had come the jewelry. Based on her dress,

Mia had chosen chandelier earrings made of real diamonds but refused the tiara.

The only jewelry she wanted was from Nikandros.

Excitement a tight knot in her gut, she let herself be pampered. Between the mud pack and the massage, she'd even napped, something her body was insisting on these days.

Blow-dried into soft waves around her face, her hair gleamed like rough silk. With Eleni's help—Mia had to draw the line at the assistants seeing her in her underwear—she got into the peach-colored ball gown they'd chosen. Her belly was visible now but the dress had voluptuous skirts that hid it quite well.

She didn't care who saw her or what they thought, but she wanted to keep an element of surprise with Nik.

An intricately ruffled bodice and a strapless push-up bra made her meager chest swell up against the heart-shaped neckline. It fell in soft folds to her ankles. Chandelier earrings at her ears picked out the hints of white in the dress, and silver strapped sandals finished her ensemble.

Staring at herself in the full-length mirror, Mia told herself to be brave.

If Nikandros had wanted a princess, it would have been easier. If he'd wanted a glamorous, accomplished wife like Brian did, even that would have been easier.

But he wanted just Mia—and everything that meant.

The Mia she'd been on the soccer field, because no one could hurt her there, the Mia she'd been before her father had fallen into his addiction, the Mia that she was discovering she could be if it meant the Daredevil Prince would be hers.

And only hers.

The party was in full swing in the ballroom by the time Nikandros arrived. He had no news from Andreas still. He'd had a meeting with the Crown Council and some other cabinet members. Assured them that everything was stable.

Even they could see the large-scale investments that Gabriel and he were planning. He hadn't shared the final plans but that was another front he'd handled for the near future.

If not for the ache in his heart, he would have celebrated.

Every morning, when he woke up, he thought Mia's absence would hurt less. That day, he wouldn't think of her every hour.

And every day, he went to bed feeling as if his heart was slowly dying.

Champagne glass in hand, he circulated among the small crowd in the ballroom. The party had been to welcome Gabriel into the fold, introduce him to some of the top businessmen in Drakon. But he'd asked Eleni to include the palace staff too.

They'd been working tirelessly with him, and Nikandros was learning he would be nothing without good staff. He strolled into one of the numerous balconies when a staffer, Louisa from Records, had approached him and pressed a note to his hand with a stiff greeting.

Frowning, he looked at the note in his hand. By the time, he opened it, she'd disappeared.

I'm twenty-one weeks old. My mama used to be a championship soccer player. If you want to know more, go to the gardens he gave her.

The note was written in a scrawly handwriting he didn't recognize. Hope punched into his throat, almost knocking him out at his knees. He finished his Champagne, handed the glass off and hurried to the gardens.

The gardens were redolent with thick fragrance.

But even in the dark night, he saw the envelope fluttering in the small window in the gazebo. Heart thundering in his ears, he flattened it with shaking hands.

My dad used to be the Daredevil Prince. But Mama says he's just a prince now and she likes him better this way. The greenhouse he built for her might have the next clue.

He hesitated only a few seconds before he made his way to the greenhouse. Another note fluttered near one of the rare orchids that Mia had lovingly coaxed into life before she had left.

His throat clenched when he saw the next note.

Mama's sad that my dad sent her away. But she says she'll not give up on her Prince. But he has to find her. Go to the place where tales of Drakon have lived for centuries.

He went to the library.
Found another note.

Mama says the Prince and she have a good start on their soccer team. Check the theater for the next note.

He went to the small theater where they'd watched soccer games with buckets of popcorn while yelling comments at the screen. He laughed so hard when he got there. The minx had sent him on a chase all over the palace, sending him to all the places where they'd spent time together.

He found another note on top of a DVD.

If you want to know if I'm a boy or a girl, go to the kitchens.

He went to the kitchens, where he'd taken her one pink dawn because she'd said she was hungry.

This time, there was a note and something more on the table where they had sat down. A small black-and-white picture, an ultrasound scan. And even he, who knew nothing about babies, could see the two tiny beans nestled against each other.

Mama says my sister gets to be the captain of the soccer team. But boys are good at soccer too, yes?

Joy made his chest ache while Nikandros dragged himself off to his suite. Dressed in a peach-colored ball gown that hugged the slim curves of her body, Mia stood in the middle of the lounge, waiting for him. Her golden skin gleamed in the lights of the chandelier, her eyes traveling over him with a joy that he knew mirrored his own.

"You took far too long," she said, and he burst out laughing.

"You took forever to come back to me," he threw back at her, greedily consuming her with his gaze. His heart was threatening to beat out of his chest so he stood at the arch, willing his emotions to calm down. If he touched her now, he would rip off that beautiful ball gown and take her with a raw, primal hunger that could even hurt her.

His gaze moved to her belly and then up. "Two, Mia?"

Tears were fluttering in her eyes as she nodded. "Two, Nikandros. And all three of us choose you. We love you."

He fell back against the wall, his knees shaking for the first time in his life. Not even on the highest cliff or the darkest night had his heart threatened to beat out of his chest like this. Never had shivers like these filled his body.

Such engulfing love filled him that he thought he couldn't draw air.

She walked toward him like a dream come true. "You're the sexiest, kindest, most wonderful man I've ever known, and I'm not giving you up without a fight.

"I want to share the good and the bad with you. I want to be your friend and lover and everything under the sky. A hundred years, an eternity and I would still choose you, Nikandros. No one could measure what you mean to me.

"I love you with my every breath, *carino*, and I only ask what you said once.

"To give us a chance. To let this grow into something more. To let me show you that you're my heart.

"I won't leave your side through anything."

He still didn't say anything. Something torturous flitted across his face.

Mia reached for him with a whimper. Fingers shaking, she traced the proud angles of his face. "Please, Nikandros. Say something. Anything. Tell me how to love you. Tell me what you need me to be, and I will. Demand what you want of me and I'll willingly give it to you.

"I have enough love for the both of us, Nik."

With a deep groan, he crushed her mouth with his.

Whispered frantic endearments that skewered the last of Mia's fears. "I had to send you away, Mia. I had to know if I would be your choice.

"It was the hardest thing I have ever done. Like breaking my own heart with my hands.

"I love you, Mia. I think I fell in love with you all those years ago, when I saw you streak through the field like a bolt of lightning.

"I believed every lie Brian told me because it would be easy to resent you.

"I will love you with everything I have, *glykia mou*. This world, Drakon, all my achievements, nothing matters without you by my side."

Tears spilled over onto her cheeks. "Sorry it took me this long to figure it out," Mia whispered, wrapping her arms tight around him.

His fingers held her tight at the base of her head, his mouth pressed tight against her temple. He showered kisses all over.

Mia shivered at the graze of his hard body, at the power contained in his lithe frame. At the desire he was unleashing with a shudder that rocked his body.

And then he went to his knees and kissed her belly, such joy shining in his eyes that Mia knew they'd make it. That she'd found her Prince, the man who'd taught her what brave meant, the man who'd taught her to love.

EPILOGUE

Seven years later

PRINCESS MIA OF DRAKON leaned back and balanced herself on her elbows to get a better view of her six-year-old twins giving their dad a run for his money with a swift kick of the football. Drakonite sun made the sandy beach nicely warm against her skin while the waves at her feet provided a cooling contrast.

Miles of beach stretched on either side, breaking against the craggy cliffs of the mountains. The water was such a gorgeous turquoise blue that it never failed to take away Mia's breath.

It was a slice of paradise. Made even more so because in seven years of marriage, it had become a private haven for her and Nik and their twins. Seven years of marriage while Nikandros settled into his role as the chief economic advisor for the Drakonite economy.

Only a week ago the project he had begun with Gabriel had reached completion. Seven long years of Nik's hard work and now Drakon reigned top as the Mediterranean's true jewel, its economy booming in the world market. And for every hour and day and night he'd spent making his vision come true, Nikandros had given Mia even more.

A loving husband, a wicked lover to this day and the best friend, a man who kept every promise he'd ever made to her and to their kids.

He didn't miss a single vacation, nor failed to notice a single one of their twins' myriad accomplishments. Between the kids and her sports charities, her life had been brimming with happiness and pride.

A shout from him tore Mia's gaze to him.

Royal blue shorts hanging low on his hips bared Nikandros's leanly defined chest. Olive skin gleamed in the sun and even at this distance, Mia could feel his gaze travel over her with a sizzling intent that made the sand rub restlessly against her damp and warm skin.

Just then, a ball came flying toward him and he barely kicked it back.

Grinning, Mia let out a whoop as Tia kicked the ball past her twin Alexio's head and toward the imaginary goal post. Leaving them to their squabble, Nikandros flopped down on the sand, rubbing one muscled thigh against hers.

The heat that flared between them was instantaneous, all-consuming.

Grasping her chin in his hand, he pressed a hot, damp kiss to her mouth. Breath hitching, Mia sank her fingers into his hair and stroked his tongue. Barely had they gotten started when the ball flew over their heads again and they fell apart, shaking and laughing.

"I told you we were turning them against each other,"

Mia complained, hearing the argument about the goal between the twins.

Gaze devilish blue, Nik only smiled. Even before he asked it, Mia knew what he was thinking. She'd insisted on waiting before they got pregnant again. Because, Prince of Drakon or not, it was hard enough to share him sometimes with their boisterous twins.

She'd wanted them to learn each other better, love each other a little more before they added to their brood.

Pushing her back into the sand, Nik palmed her almost-flat midriff, his gaze intense. "Remember how we talked about our own team?"

Mia nodded, breathless like a teenager again. Breathless in the rush of his love, still. Always breathless, he made Mia feel like she was the center of his world. Nothing—no man or politics or thrill—would ever take him away from her.

Fingers trembling at the surge of love that filled her, Mia pushed back the hair that flopped onto his forehead. "Yes, Nikandros, I'm ready."

"Tonight then, *pethi mou*? After the midnight swim?"

She laughed, nodded and then pushing herself upward, pressed her mouth to his. "It's a date, *carino*."

* * * * *

If you enjoyed the first part of Tara Pammi's
THE DRAKON ROYALS *trilogy,*
look out for the second instalment—
coming June 2017!

In the meantime, why not enjoy these
other great Tara Pammi stories...
MARRIED FOR THE SHEIKH'S DUTY
THE SURPRISE CONTI CHILD
THE UNWANTED CONTI BRIDE
THE SHEIKH'S PREGNANT PRISONER
BOUGHT FOR HER INNOCENCE
Available now!

#3525 THE FORCED BRIDE OF ALAZAR
Seduced by a Sheikh
by Kate Hewitt
Azim al Bahjat stuns Alazar with his return to his kingdom and must claim his betrothed. Beguiling Johara's every instinct is to run. But as he shows her how intoxicating their wedding night could be, she begins to consider surrender...

#3526 THE INNOCENT'S SHAMEFUL SECRET
Secret Heirs of Billionaires
by Sara Craven
Alexis Constantinou haunts Selena Blake's every memory—she dreams every night of the scorching affair that stole her innocence. Seeing Alexis again, Selena cannot ignore their passion—but does she dare reveal the truth she's hidden? The secret Constantinou heir!

#3527 BLACKMAILED DOWN THE AISLE
by Louise Fuller
Billionaire Rollo Fleming catches Daisy Maddox sneaking into his office and demands she become the wife he needs for a business deal! With every kiss, Daisy's guard melts, and she discovers *pleasurable* advantages to being blackmailed down the aisle...

#3528 THE ITALIAN'S VENGEFUL SEDUCTION
Claimed by a Billionaire
by Bella Frances
Marco Borsatto gave Stacey her first taste of pleasure...only to accuse her of betrayal. She refuses to be hurt again and Marco isn't a man to forgive. But when he rescues her, it reignites an electrifying magnetism they never fully explored...

YOU CAN FIND MORE INFORMATION ON UPCOMING HARLEQUIN® TITLES, FREE EXCERPTS AND MORE AT WWW.HARLEQUIN.COM.

HPCNM0417RB

*Persuading plain Jane to marry him was easy enough—
but Sheikh Zayed Al Zawba hadn't bargained on the
irresistible curves hidden under her clothes or that she
is deliciously untouched. When Jane begins to tempt
him beyond his wildest dreams, leaving their marriage
unconsummated becomes impossible...*

Read on for a sneak preview of
Sharon Kendrick's book
THE SHEIKH'S BOUGHT WIFE.

Wedlocked!
Conveniently wedded, passionately bedded!

It was difficult to be distant when her body seemed to have
developed a stubborn will of its own. When she found herself
wanting to push her aching breasts against Zayed's powerful
chest as he caught her in his arms for the traditional first
dance between bride and groom. As it was, she could barely
think straight and wasn't it the most infuriating thing in the
world that he immediately seemed to pick up on that?

"You seem to be having trouble breathing, dear wife,"
he murmured as he moved her to the center of the marble
dance floor.

"The dress is very tight."

"I'd noticed." He twirled her around, holding her back a
little. "It looks very well on you."

She forced a tight smile but she didn't relax. "Thank
you."

"Or maybe it is the excitement of having me this close to
you which is making you pant like a little kitten?"

"You're annoying me, rather than exciting me. And I do wish you'd stop trying to get underneath my skin."

"Don't you like people getting underneath your skin, Jane?"

"No," she said honestly. "I don't."

"Why not?"

She met the blaze of his ebony eyes and suppressed a shiver. "Does everything have to have a reason?"

"In my experience, yes." There was a pause. "Has a man hurt you in the past?"

This was her chance to tell him yes—even though the very idea that someone had got that close to her was laughable.

Zayed had already guessed she might be a virgin, but that didn't even come close to her shameful lack of experience.

Trying to ignore the way his groin was brushing against her as he edged her closer, she glanced up at him, her cheeks burning. "I refuse to answer that on the grounds that I might incriminate myself. Tell me instead, do you always insist on interrogating women when you're dancing with them?"

"No. I don't," he said simply. "But then I've never had a bride before and I've never danced with a woman who was so determined not to give anything of herself away."

"And that's the only reason you want to know," she said quietly. "Because you like a challenge."

"All men like a challenge, Jane." His black eyes gleamed. "Haven't you learned that by now?"

She didn't answer—because how was she qualified to answer any questions about what men did or didn't like?

Don't miss
THE SHEIKH'S BOUGHT WIFE,
available May 2017 wherever
Harlequin Presents® books and ebooks are sold.

www.Harlequin.com

HARLEQUIN

Presents®

**Next month, look out for *Bound by the Sultan's Baby*
by Carol Marinelli—a story of a scandalous royal
consequence and a billionaire determined
to stake his claim!**

One night with innocent wedding planner Gabi was all
Sultan Alim al-Lehan allowed himself. But when duty
dictates he must marry, memories of their forbidden
pleasure prove impossible to forget—especially when he
discovers Gabi has just returned from maternity leave!

The baby *must* be his, but if Gabi won't tell him, Alim
will seduce the truth out of her! Commanding she
arrange his wedding, even if he's not yet picked a wife,
is the ideal ruse. Alim wants her in his bed but must
decide—will she be a sultan's mistress or bride?

Don't miss

BOUND BY THE SULTAN'S BABY

Available May 2017

Stay Connected:

www.Harlequin.com

 /HarlequinBooks

@HarlequinBooks

 /HarlequinBooks

HP06063